STITCH IN SNOW

ANNE McCAFFREY
STITCH IN SNOW

TOR

A TOM DOHERTY ASSOCIATES BOOK

STITCH IN SNOW

Copyright © 1984 by Anne McCaffrey

Reprinted by arrangement with Brandywyne Books

A TOR Book

Published by Tom Doherty Associates
8-10 West 36 Street
New York, N.Y. 10018

First TOR printing: May 1985

ISBN: 0-312-93753-9

Printed in the United States of America

*Affectionately dedicated
to
Sheila, Mic and Eric Simonson
and the feline complement of their house*

STITCH IN SNOW

I

"You've got problems, Dana Jane Lovell," said my friend Mairead, unexpectedly grim. She took the newly finished Arran sweater, size 40, absently running her fingers over the pattern before she placed it with indifferent care on the counter.

"Whatever do you mean?"

Mairead's ugly-attractive face screwed into a grimace of distaste.

"That's the second sweater this month."

"So?"

11

"So," she took me by the upper arm, started me towards the door of her tourist boutique, calling over her shoulder, "Sally, watch the shop. I'll be in the other office."

She marched me out to the street, ignoring my protests that I did not want a drink at this hour of the morning, and pulled me ruthlessly towards the pub across the little square, her 'other office.'

"Hush yourself, Dana, you've been worrying over Tim again."

"I am not worried about Tim. At 20 my son is old enough to take care of himself . . ."

"Which is your problem, because he isn't here for you to take care of."

"Mairead!" I jerked my arm out of her grip. "You know I'm not that kind of mother."

"I didn't say you were," she snapped back, her brown eyes sparkling so fiercely that, in spite of having known her tempestuous moods for five years, I was a bit daunted. "I said that you miss having him, or someone, to take care of. You're that sort, no matter what else you are and do!"

She took my arm again, her fingers biting into my flesh, and hauled me the rest of the distance to the pub. At eleven-fifteen on a bright Thursday morning in November, the pub was empty. Declan, the barman, was busy elsewhere for we could hear his cheerful whistle.

"When you're ready, Declan," Mairead sang out as she gestured me to take a bar stool. "I know you're not that sort of mother, Dana, and I respect you for it. But the fact remains that you're miserable.''

"I am not.''

"Oh, yes, you are,'' and she wangled a finger at me, her eyes still snapping. "Two Arrans in one month!'' She made a noise of utter disgust.

"You keep saying that you'll take all I can knit for you.''

Mairead is dramatic and now she raised her eyes and hands heavenwards for patience.

"Look, get away from the knitting needles. Get out of that house for a break. Go see your London publisher, your agent. Go to Paris, you said you've always wanted to go . . .''

"I can't go anywhere right now . . .''

"I'll mind the house for you, and the dog, and the mail . . .''

"That's not the problem. I'm writing . . .''

"Then stop! Go away! Meet people! Get involved . . .''

"That's fine advice while I'm away and involved and meeting people, but it doesn't do anything for me when I have to come back, to take care of my house, my dog, my mail and finish my book. So what if I'm knitting a lot, there's nothing on TV right now that I care to watch and . . .''

The impetus of her attack faltered and her shoulders sagged a bit, admitting the logic of my refutation. She pulled her mouth down, glaring about the room under wrinkled brows. She'd need to pluck them

13

again, I noticed. Then she reached for her cigarettes, glaring at me to forestall my inevitable protest. She did try to cut down on smoking in my presence.

"I'm coping, Mairead. I admit you've got a point. I am lonely. More so this year than last. Although I can't understand why I should miss Tim more now than when he first started college. . . ."

In one of her mercurial changes, Mairead grinned at me, and chuckled in her earthy way. "Should I remind you about Peter-pet?"

"No."

"What'll it be, ladies?" asked the cheerful voice of Declan, the barman, emerging from his back premises. He twitched at the overlong sleeves of his shirt to get the cuffs above his wrists and rested his hands on the counter. Declan had been a jockey until a horse had come down on him in a hurdle race, fracturing his pelvis in a number of barely mendable pieces. He was a favorite of ours, especially since his racing tips were eighty percent reliable. Tim had worked that out on his calculator over a month's betting performance.

We ordered lager and lime. Mairead absently reminding Declan to make it Carlsberg, while he reproachfully reminded her that he never forgot her preference. He poured the ale, leaving sufficient space in the glasses for the lime cordial, placed the bottles on the bar for us to suit ourselves, and went on about his business. He had an unerring instinct for knowing when you wanted to chat him up or be left alone.

"Peter did fill a void . . . Whoops! Sorry about

14

that, pet," said Mairead the irrepressible. "He was good for you in some ways," she went on, in a pensive mood, turning her lager glass so that the wet bottom made damp circles on the bar wood. "But he sure wasn't a permanent answer for you."

"I don't want a permanent answer," I said. "Peter was in many ways just what I needed. . . ."

"You sure as hell were what he needed," Mairead can never suppress her jaundices. "A mother figure! Christ, what is it with this country's men? They'll either charm your pockets bare or they're grown up little boys creeping back into the womb! Sick of 'em! That's what I am! Sick of the whole lot of 'em."

"I . . ."

She whirled before I got another syllable out, her finger under my nose. "And don't you dare say I've tried the lot of 'em!"

"Oh, ho and have you?"

"Never you mind about me, Dana Jane Lovell. I can and do take care of myself. It's *you* I'm worried about. You gave Peter-pet the boot last May . . ." her voice altered from stern to amused, "just in time for Tim to come home to a pure household. It's November now and it's not fair on you. Mind, I'm not saying you should find another Peter and slough him off next April again, *but* you do need someone about for a while."

I was both annoyed and amused by Mairead. Amused because she was so intense about sorting out my life to her satisfaction, never mind about mine; and annoyed because she felt her solution would suit me. Annoyed also because she so acutely identified my malaise: a restlessness I had refused to admit to myself. However, standing in the way of any candid admission were my principles, or perhaps, just a large pride.

From the onset of the lung cancer which killed him, my husband, Ray, had withdrawn from much physical contact with me. It had taken him two years to die, fighting every day to keep alive. His courage, his humor, his wisdom in the face of death had endeared him far more to me than any physical relationship. After his death I had gone about in a sort of numb shock, and then, while I was in graduate school, I found solace in the arms of a fellow student. I even considered marrying Ross, but something had restrained me. Much later I realized that it had been because Ross couldn't measure up to the standards Ray had set. Specious, perhaps, but I saw no reason, then, or since, to compromise. I think that was a basic difference between Mairead and myself. She could, would and did compromise, enjoying a relationship for what merit it had, then severing it, sometimes rather brutally, when something about the relationship displeased her.

Physical needs don't appreciate esoteric principles. So I was left, holding a bag of knitting.

Mairead argued and threatened me for the better part of an hour, getting so fraught herself that she departed, swearing she wouldn't take another sweater

off my hands for six months, so I needn't waste my
time running up another one. She wouldn't buy it for
all the gold in the country: she'd be selling dangerous
goods. Who wanted a sex-starved sweater, reeking of
frustrations, strong enough to haunt the purchaser and
she'd be to blame, she would!

One of our whimsies is her sales pitch on the Arran
jumpers I knit for her: they're made by a little (I'm
5' 5", white-haired lady (my once carroty hair, bane
of my existence as a young girl, has plenty of silver
streaks), living in a gatelodge in County Wicklow.

To this gatelodge I repaired, having solved nothing
except the disposition of an hour, and sixty-nine pence
on lager and lime.

I tried to stimulate the sense of pleasure I usually
have when I see my pleasant abode, framed by a
stand of magnificent beeches and the estate wall. The
gatelodge is a gem, complete with an enclosed garden
of about a half acre. I was extraordinarily lucky to
have acquired its lease, a fringe benefit of being an
author. With gothic wooden trim on its peaked roofs,
the lodge was also like a Gothic L-cross, the leg
being a new addition with a modern kitchen and
bathroom. The top cross piece contained the hall and
two small bedrooms, the living room was the shaft.
There was a lovely big fireplace in the living room
which, in theory, heated the house. The wall to the
left of the fireplace was covered with shelves for my
books and record collection with a special drawer for
the hi-fi and tape recorder. The stairs to the single

upstairs room were on the wall opposite the fireplace. My garret, which had a more modest fireplace, was the only one in the attic and took up the whole gable area. The vaulted ceiling gave me a glorious feeling of having more space than I actually did. Two windows gave views of meadows and mountains, pleasant for unfocused looking-at during moments of inspirational gazing.

The kitchen was small but, as the landlord had been remodelling it (I hate to think what it *had* been for my first glimpse had been bare walls and floor) when I took the lease so I had a chance to make it more efficient, adding a few things at my own expense when Mr. Hengarty muttered darkly about costs. We were both pleased with the result. I had a countertop range, for one thing, space for an almost American size fridge/freezer, an under-the-counter washing machine, good working and shelf space. The bathroom was also small but had a bathtub with shower attachments and the hot water heater was topped by a good linen press. Irish houses do not run to American-style closets so I connived with Mr. Hengarty's carpenter to build me some in both the small bedrooms and my office-bedroom. We were right and tight in my little houseen, on a long lease. Mr. Hengarty could brag about his American author tenant and I generally paid the rent on time.

Tim had cut me a vegetable garden the first year so we had fresh produce and the original tenant's fruit trees were mature and bore generously. Right now, everything in the garden was bare, including my response to it all as I parked my Peugeot on the black-top beside my empty house.

I sat for a long time in the car, in a limbo of sorts, like Christopher Robin, halfway up the stairs. I've often felt that a car is that sort of mid-point. I do a lot of good thinking while I drive, suspended between point A and point B, especially when I don't want to stand on either point. I could think about my problem—loneliness—more objectively in the car than I could in the house where the absence of someone to care for, namely my son Tim, would be palpable. I had missed him last year, but I had been enjoying an amusing affair with Peter Neville, one which I'd hoped would mature into a lasting relationship. Peter had been my plane seatmate from New York to Dublin on my return from a lecture tour I'd done after winning a young adult fiction award for one of my 'Timmy' books. Peter was employed as a film editor for RTE though he never seemed to spend much time editing anything, except his funny stories. He'd been very good company, amusing, witty, inventive, charming . . . most of the time. When 'drink taken,' as the phrase goes, he underwent an alarming metamorphosis. Admittedly, he could hold enormous quantities of drink before the switch occurred. It was during one of those infrequent episodes that I broke off our relationship, at the top of my lungs, afterwards regretting far more that he had goaded me into losing my temper than that he had departed.

19

Tim had come home soon afterward for the summer and his presence had satisfied that home-making instinct in me that defies the independence of mind and discipline of the body.

Mairead can tease me unmercifully about my maternal instinct, my deplorable (her adjective) need to succor the friendless, hungry and selfish. Fond as I am of Mairead, I could not be as hard and cynical as she, however much that would protect me from my impulses and trusting nature.

I didn't want another entanglement like the one I'd had with Peter Neville which had posed more problems than it solved. Mairead had accused me of having a distorted recollection of my married life with Ray before he took ill: she said I couldn't compare all men with an idealized Ray.

"No man could be as nice as that Raymond of yours," she'd said in disgust one night when I'd tried valiantly to explain the respect we'd shared, the gentleness and kindness of the man. "Furthermore, once you'd rubbed together a few years longer, you'd have rubbed against each other, too. He died before you lost him."

She could be right, I'd thought privately, having seen other 'ideal' marriages disintegrate. But Ray had been different. My memories of our brief years together could not be tarnished by the wisp of any doubt.

Memory is, unfortunately, cold comfort in bed, or cold company in a lonely house.

Circumstance, in the form of a letter from my publisher outlining another lecture tour for March and April, raised its charming head. I welcomed the opportunity because it solved so many problems and laid to rest all current doubts. I'd be visiting 24 cities in six weeks—rather a stiff program, but I'd have weekends clear and generally at the publisher's expense. I'd be able to stay with my sister in New York and visit Ray's sister in Berkeley, and that marvelous children's librarian in Pittsburgh. There were other people I could visit but sometimes, on such a busy schedule, it was wiser to retire gratefully to the impersonal room of a hotel and regroup one's energies. The letter asked many questions about my wishes on the tour.

I phoned Mairead to tell her I was taking her advice about travelling.

"Weaseled out of it again, have you?" she replied. "Mind now, I still won't take another Arran off you."

"I won't have time. I've got letters and lectures to write and this novel to finish."

And I didn't have time to knit again until March when I took off for New York. To relieve the tedium of 7½ hours flying time, I cast on the border of a size 44 Arran pullover.

II

II

In New York City, I generally put up with my sister, Suzanne. And I use the term 'put up' advisedly. Her apartment, a pleasant one between Amsterdam and Columbus in the mid-eighties, is convenient even if I do have to share a bedroom with my niece. Veronica is a very pretty child who is unfortunately afflicted with adenoids. Suzie has a 'thing' about American hospitals and wouldn't dream of subjecting her precious daughter to their brutalities. I make no comment. My nephew, James, at sixteen is far more streetwise

25

than Suzie realizes, and is very supercilious about anything except money. He has been trying for the past three years to find out how much money I earn. I like my brother-in-law, Tom. He's a courteous man, a considerate father and a conscientious husband and nowhere near the dolt Suzie makes him out. I marvel at his fortitude for I have never seen him flinch nor ever heard him respond to Suzie's steady stream of derogatory remarks and reproaches. On those few occasions when Suzie has been out at one of her meetings, Tom and I have enjoyed our conversations for I have never found him limited to accountancy and high finance as Suzie complains.

Fortunately, with legitimate business engagements, I don't have to spend much time in the apartment, though this causes Suzie to whinge about the fact that I never seem to spend *any* time with my only blood relatives. If Tom who has to live with her can endure her bitching, I remind myself firmly that Suzie and I were extremely close as sisters, growing up with loving, concerned parents, in a home as secure as only Midwest America can make one. I do privately wonder where the metamorphosis in her took place. Now we have nothing in common except that childhood which is inadequate to support contact for more than a few days a year.

My agent, on the other hand, is the sort of friend who picks up where you both left off the last time you met, as if there had been no months or years intervening. Sam and I often have rather expensive long distance phone calls, sorting out contracts and manuscripts, but he has remained unchanged by his considerable success in the field, and highly amused by mine. Sam and I shared space at the same table in Hazen's coffee shop in Harvard Square where he expostulated with pungent wit on the state of Lit'rachure. He had been vocally prominent in the literary circles at Harvard and fancied himself a critic in the style of George Bernard Shaw. After graduation he had demeaned himself by joining a literary agency ("The only job I could get with a Harvard degree."), had taken a chance on several unknown authors and lucked out, as he now has the humility to admit. He had just opened his own agency when the first of my 'Timmy' books were accepted so I had approached him to represent me. He had a good laugh, since juveniles were not what he usually deigned to handle, but he read the manuscript and genuinely liked it . . . in spite of his more mature and literate tastes, as he put it. I have never regretted approaching Sam and he has shrewdly managed my literary affairs ever since.

I don't really like starting off a tour in New York City. It has a surfeit of book signings, author-interviews and press parties. I much prefer smaller cities with small convenient airports, but New York is the Big Smoke. This year my publisher was cooperating with the B. Dalton chain: last year had been Walden's turn. Both know how to organize signings, with attentive staff, a well-situated table, plenty of pens, a good window display and dumper boxes near the table.

Signings, for someone like myself, very low league, occur at the lunch hour when the most possible number of impulse buyers and browsers can be tempted to purchase a copy of The Book for the bonus of having a 'signed' copy. It is also very gratifying when loyal readers, hearing of your visit, come especially to get a new book signed or just to chat. A writer is a solitary person, despite the image generally projected about wining, dining and conniving with fellow authors. Consequently getting to meet the people who read your books provides very salutary feed-back.

That morning several unusual incidents alleviated the awkwardness of sitting, in wait, as Timmy puts it, for victims. I have to presume that I have a capable air about me, pen in hand, for two ladies in their middle years came up to me and inquired, rather starchily, what had happened to Stouffer's. Before I remembered that the new Dalton Fifth Avenue store occupied the old Stouffer premises, the manager answered the question. There was a definite accusation of me in the expressions of the two disappointed lunchers. Then a smallish gentleman, in a raincoat with a rolled up newspaper under his arm and an umbrella in his other hand, approached the table, his expression anxious.

"I can't find my book," he told me plaintively but not accusatorily.

"What are you looking for?" the manager asked, taking over the burden.

He glanced at her as if not certain she had addressed him.

"Oh, it's medical."

"That would be downstairs."

He trudged off.

A well dressed gentleman then appeared before us, looking confused. He demanded to know what I had done to Stouffer's. Once again the manager intervened with the explanation that Stouffer's had closed down.

"But what am I to do?" This time his soft southern accent was apparent. He kept looking over his shoulder, disturbed by the presence of so many books where he had expected tables and food.

"Were you meeting someone?"

"Of course not," he replied, somewhat irritable. "But Stouffer's is the only food that agrees with me here." 'Here' came out 'hyeah' and his condemnation of New York restaurants was patent.

"Schrafft's . . ."

"Schrafft's?" He gave her the most disgusted stare for her impudent suggestion and then, inclining his head to me as if exonerating my part in the disappearance of his favorite eatery, he swept away.

We were stifling our amusement when our medical book friend returned, his anxiety bordering total desolation.

"I can't find my book."

I caught the emphasis before the others. "You mean, you've published a medical book?"

"Yes, yes. And I was told it was on display here. Today is its publication day!" He was woebegone.

I quite understood his dejection.

"Now, then," said the manager soothingly, stepping around to him. "I'm sure we'll find it on the new books rack. If you'll just come with me, Mr. . . ."

I don't recall his name but his expression had definitely lightened at the manager's helpfulness and he trailed off after her with all the confidence of the found child.

My hour of autographing was nearly over when a woman came dashing in, and straight up to me at my table.

"Oh, dear, have you seen Marjorie? She promised to meet me at Stouffer's but you've moved it so I don't know where she will . . ." She glanced past me just then, "Marjorie! Do you mean to tell me you've been in *here* looking at *books* all the time *I've* been out *there* . . ." She hauled her delinquent friend away.

"I am *not* going to be lunching you at Stouffer's," my editor informed me and we all broke up laughing.

I had a predictable, if competent interview at a radio station, signing a book for the producer's thirteen-year-old son whose birthday was coming soon. When I got back to Suzie's, she was out, so I had time to write up the incident in my 'brains.' That's what Timmy calls my diary and I must say it has proved invaluable to record such trivia on a tour. I did two school libraries the next day and a Literary Circle.

Fortunately no one insisted that I look at their manuscript. Sam had finally got *that* across. And that was that for New York City.

The next day I took Amtrak down to Washington where the tour would start in earnest with a two day stint of library groups at morning coffees, lunchtime salads and afternoon teas. The first morning I had an early TV appearance and, as I had not yet caught up to American time, I wanted to get a good night's rest. I shared a cab—a Washington habit—with a French speaking couple who were left off at Watergate Hotel. It's silly of me to ascribe to a mere building the faults that occur within it but I was very glad to drive away from that infamous area.

As I was checking in, a very attractive woman in a green velvet pants suit was arguing with the other reservations clerk. She was certain that her agent had booked her a room which she needed only for the night. As I was handed my room key, she was told the price of the accommodation. "I want to sleep in it for one night, not purchase it outright!" she exclaimed with justifiable exasperation.

I had great sympathy for her for she looked tired and strained. I had been in her situation when you long for the solitude of a room and a soothing bath. Her comment was good enough to be inscribed in my 'brains' which I did as I enjoyed a leisurely meal in my room in front of the TV, and then phoned Tim to bring him up to date. I never call him from Suzie's as she expects me to tell her 'all.'

31

I was more than a little amused, therefore, to find
the lady at the TV station the next morning. She
vaguely recognized me as people accustomed to being
in public notice will do: I got a pleasant half smile
and the raising of eyebrows acknowledging the fleet-
ing memory. She looked considerably rested so she
must have taken the room, whatever the cost. While
waiting to be called, we exchanged pleasantries, avoiding names. I watched her segment of the Breakfast
Program and she was promoting her autobiography of
years spent in Hollywood. I heard her name and I
should have jotted it down but I didn't and it had
escaped my overloaded 'forgettery' by the time I got
back to my hotel room.

By the third lecture on the first day, I began to
worry about repeating myself too glibly. You fall into
a sort of pattern, answering questions, fending off
others, and sometimes you neglect to make the one
point you know you should have emphasized. At the
end of the second day, however, I was back into the
rhythm and as I relaxed on the train to Philadelphia, I
could tote up the day's events in my 'brains' and not
feel any twinges of omissions. In Philadelphia I had
another two days of library dates, luncheons, radio
and a newspaper interview with the children's editor
of the Sunday paper. Then I was on the plane to
Boston.

Boston's a good town for me. I like what the City
Fathers have done to refurbish a town which I remember from college days as scruffy and impossibly dowdy.

Mind you, they've done little about the clapboard in grey or the wretched mud-brown which they insist on painting residences. I could be blindfolded and suddenly released in the outskirts of Boston and recognize it instantly. Still Boston has lobster dinners and two of my closest college friends so I could anticipate a good time: one working day before the Sunday off with Jean and Pota.

After Boston, there was the pleasure of seeing my most favorite children's librarian, Alma Fairing, in Pittsburgh. Any engagements in that city are spiced with her scintillating wit, association with her marvellous family and *gallant* husband. If she hadn't been Alma and my favorite librarian. . . .

Once I left Pittsburgh, the tour would descend into 50-minute evening plane trips to the next city, village or hamlet in which I was to speak, dazzle, charm new readers and gratify old friends. By Detroit, I had to list in my 'brains' that my digestion was showing the effects of travel. And I kept arriving at each new hotel to find BUTCH CASSIDY AND THE SUNDANCE KID being shown on TV. "Who is that guy?" seemed to be the cue line for my entrance to my night's hotel room. The coincidence was a joke which only I could enjoy. It would take too long to explain it all to each successive bellboy. I noted the 'haunting' in my 'brains.'

Chicago was freezing cold with its icy wind about to cut the unwary in two. I'm used to wind in Ireland. I keep saying that I live in hurricane alley with Gale

Anne McCaffrey

Force 8 and 9 winds a matter of daily occurrence. Chicago's wind has its own ferocity and knife edge. I despise O'Hare airport. And on the way through the security arch, they stopped me for my knitting needles! Chicago was also marred by an odious man who had ogled me through my solitary dinner in the hotel and before I could avoid him, wanted me to join him in the bar 'for drinks . . . and afters.' His 'afters' were fully explained by his leer. I made a majestic retreat and then wrote a full description of him into my 'brains.' The next time I needed a sleazy character I'd use him. He'd never recognize himself from an accurate description: that sort never do. When that was inscribed to my satisfaction, I flipped on the TV and got "Who is that guy?" I flicked it off and phoned Tim. He was in one of his funny moods and no TV show could compare with my son in a high good humor.

Milwaukee, Minneapolis, St. Louis and Kansas City rolled past and I had to spend my 50-minute flights making entries in my diary before I forgot relevant and useful details which would make the next tour easier. That is, if there was a next tour. I was seriously doubting that when we took off from Kansas City for Denver.

I phoned Tim every night, to keep my reality, and in Kansas City, I had the oddest sensation that there was something he was dying to tell me, but was held back.

I turned to my knitting on the Denver flight, as

much to soothe my travel-logged spirit as to ignore the ominous clouds through which the airplane passed. One thing about air travel, you're apt to see the sun for a while, just so you know what it does look like in wintry March.

Our landing at Denver was not exactly perilous although the snow clung to the viewports. But if you have been flying as much as I had been, you can detect the subtle differences in a bumpy good landing and a skiddy dangerous one. The crew were all smiles as they disembarked us, advising us to wait in the lounge for flight information. As delayed flights are the inevitable consequence of nature's lofty disdain for Progress, I settled myself down in a corner of the lounge with my knitting, to observe my fellow travellers held in durance vile by a blizzard. There was a long queue at the phones. I had no one to call and no urgencies to resolve.

III

"DROPPED ANY GOOD STITCHES LATELY?" a quiet male voice asked.

I was so startled that I dropped some, gasping, looking up and letting the knitting bag slide from my lap all at the same moment.

"I'm sorry. I didn't mean to startle you," the man said, swiftly bending to pick the bag up off the floor. He began to brush it off, because the floor was dampened by people dripping snow and mud as they prowled restlessly about the airport lounge.

"Not to worry," I said, holding my hand out to retrieve my belongings. I smiled at him because his face was somewhat familiar although I couldn't place where on God's green earth we'd met. I was reminded of my encounter with the lady in the green velvet pants suit although the positions were reversed. And he was distinguished-looking, with his silvered hair and an attractively unsilvered moustache. In my perusal of my fellow travellers, I had noticed him pacing the corridors, waiting impatiently for his turn at the phone, like everyone else stranded unexpectedly in snowbound Denver.

"Is there much damage?" he asked, settling into the seat beside me as he handed back the bag.

"No," I assured him, laughing at his contrite expression and racking my brain to think where I'd seen him before as I quickly caught up the dropped stitches.

"You do that deftly. I've been admiring your skill for some time now." He grinned with all the ease of long-established acquaintanceship.

"Have you now?" I demurred. I longed for a chance to pull out my 'brains' and see if I could joggle my faulty memory.

"Yes. I can perceive that this is more than knit-one-purl-one. Ah," and he'd taken the rib edge of the sweater front and held it out. "Arran!" He sounded surprised, and fingered the wool. "And báinan, too."

"You're Irish?" He'd neither the brogue nor the cultivated English of the well-educated Irish but few

American males would know that the oiled wool was called báinan.

"No, but I've travelled there frequently."

"Do I know you from Dublin then?" I asked, determined to establish his identity.

"Dublin?" Halfway to a frown, his eyebrows paused and his expression cleared. His eyes began to twinkle. They were a kind of serge blue, I noticed in the all-too-glaring light of the overhead fluorescents. "No, we haven't met in Dublin."

"Please, I've met so many people in the past three weeks, I plead overload."

"Does it distress you that you can't place our . . . ah . . . introduction?"

"Well, yes, sort of. I mean, it's good public relations to remember names and I've a good score so far this trip . . ."

"I wouldn't want to ruin that." His eyes twinkled more and a smile tugged at the corners of his well-shaped mouth which the moustache outlined rather than hid. *He* was enjoying my discomfiture.

"To tell the truth and shame the devil, I can't remember where we met."

"I'm the anonymous sort," he said, feigning petulance. I gave him a very severe look for he had a strong face, attractive rather than handsome, but eye-catching with his coloring.

"Not with that hair, those brows and that coffee-strainer . . ."

41

He laughed at my acerbic tone, crossing his legs and settling himself more comfortably.

"Maybe if you knit a few rows, it'll all come back. When I first saw you, you were just starting it."

"You were on the plane from Dublin?"

"No," and he looked abashed. "Not from Dublin. But this is surely the front . . ." for I was obviously dividing to make the neckline.

I had to trace back the progress of this sweater. "I did start the front on the plane from Philadelphia. Were you on the Pittsburgh flight?"

He nodded, as pleased as I was with the recognition. He leaned forward then, extending his hand. "I'll have to confess: we have never been formally introduced. We seem to have had the same itinerary."

With relief I shook his hand, my memory now dredging up a tall, faintly familiar man going through the Milwaukee security check just ahead of me.

"I don't think you saw me out of Philadelphia. You were, as usual, knitting. I had the aisle seat in front of you. You were ahead of me going through the security arch in Chicago. Remember? They held you up for the knitting needles."

"Yes, but what they expected me to be smuggling along with my knitting, I can't guess. Explosives don't come . . ." and I held up my hands a needle-length apart.

"You don't look the type to be knitting either," he said unexpectedly. "Sweetening up the husband with a handknit?"

42

"No husband."

"Boyfriend?"

"At my age? Unlikely!"

He gave me a mock-wicked smirk. "No lover?"

I laughed at his incorrigibility. "No, I do it for commercial reasons only. Knitting, I mean." At my hurried qualifier, for he had a devilish quick mind and a quicker gleam of humor, he laughed again. Someone trying to nap across the aisle from us grumbled and irritably shifted position.

"No, I knit," I said in a firm no-nonsense tone, "because I enjoy working with my hands. I've a friend who runs a small boutique in Enniskerry. She buys anything I'll make for her. Knitting's like a tranquillizer. The RAF pilots were encouraged to knit argyle socks during the War, you know, to relax."

"I didn't know." He wasn't teasing me. His attention was focused on my hands because I'd picked up all the dropped stitches and progressed further in the pattern. "How do you remember when to switch?"

I glanced down at the row. "The pattern has a simple progression in each stitch."

"Do you always work the same pattern?"

This was a rather absurd conversation for two intelligent people to be having, when one of them is a man, but it would pass the time in a snowbound airport lounge.

"Rarely. That's one of the joys of knitting Arran: the combinations are infinite."

43

I was cabling just then, knitting into the back to twist which isn't as difficult as it looks.

"You must have eyes in your fingers," he said with exasperation. "What's this pattern?"

"Lobster claw. This is the Tree of Life: that zigzag is sort of the ups and downs of marriage . . ." The subtle alteration of his mouth and the slight narrowing of his eyes suggested to me that his marriage was probably in stress just then. "The real Arran sweater tells a tale: in the west country each family had a distinctive pattern. One way to identify drowned fishermen was by the sweater pattern."

"Grisly!" He affected a shudder.

I agreed. "Some patterns are for good luck, too."

"How many of *them* were dragged up from the deep six?"

I shrugged and kept on working the pattern, glancing up at the windows against which the snow kept beating as the wind lashed and swirled outside. We'd been grounded for close to two hours and the earlier hysteria of the stranded passengers had now been replaced with resignation. I was in no bind—as yet— because my next lecture date, in Portland, Oregon, was three days away. I had planned to check into the motel and just rest up because I'd be pretty pushed by the engagements on the West Coast until Easter weekend.

I could just as well lounge around Denver as Portland. And it was reasonably obvious that I'd be staying at least overnight in Denver. Since the airlines would have to foot the hotel bill, I couldn't object.

My fellow-traveller and I sat in companionable silence while I worked nine rows, finishing that side of the neck. Then he caught my hand as I turned the sweater to start the right side. I spread the work out and he grinned as he traced the various patterns.

"No mistakes," he said, teasing me with a mock condescending tone.

"I do make 'em."

"How do you hide 'em?"

"I don't as a rule. I rip out the work . . ." He looked dismayed. "Oh, once in a while, like in this moss stitch, an irregularity won't be too noticeable. And sometimes I catch the error in the next row and just drop and redo that stitch . . ."

The p.a. system gave a high-hum burp and the disembodied voice announced with insincere regret the cancellation of all flights. Would on-going passengers please come to the accommodation desks of their respective airlines?

"I'd expected that," he said. "Were you going on?"

"Yes, but I've a three-day leeway which I'd intended to take in Portland!"

"With friends?"

"No. I just wanted to be by myself for a bit. Too much talk and rich food, too many parties and too many drinks."

"Too many faces you can't remember names for?"
His eyes twinkled.

"That's unfair. We never were introduced. Which
reminds me, I still don't have your name?"

He chuckled, a dirty low-down chuckle. "I didn't
give it!" And he knew perfectly well he hadn't.

I began to get irritated then. After all, he had
initiated the conversation, I hadn't.

"Call me Dan . . ."

"Dan, Dan, the Mystery Man?" I said, laughing to
cover my start of surprise. He couldn't know my
name: I didn't even have initials on my attaché case.

"I don't know *your* name."

"True, you don't," and grinned at him, hesitating
as he had done but with an honest reason. If I told
him my first name, he might well think I was putting
him on. I gave myself a mental kick in the pants. One
of the fringe liabilities of these lecture tours is that
you can acquire an inflated and unreal opinion of
yourself, 'fame' and 'public.' Granted my books for
children are well known, and considering his twinge
at the marriage zig-zag, he might have children who
read my books. I was so fed up with being a Visiting
Celebrity that I wanted to preserve my anonymity. I
gave him my middle name. "I'm Jane."

"Jane? Plain Jane? Me Tarzan, you Jane . . ." He
screwed up his face in comic rejection of both cli-
chés. "No, you're not plain Jane, or Tarzan Jane. I
don't even believe you are a Jane. You don't look the
type. I'll call you Jenny! On your feet, Jenny."

I swung my wool Clodagh cloak to my shoulders with a practiced twist of the wrist which he admired with a grin. "Attaché case, yes: knitting bag, no. And neither really go with that cloak . . . shopping basket more like, little green Riding Hood."

"You fail to see the subterfuge," I told him, mock haughty. "The cloak hides the knitting bag so no one knows my vice."

"Since when are knitting bags subversive?"

"Since women's lib," I said in a stage whisper, glancing about as if fearful of being overheard.

"Ah, so!"

As we made our way towards the United Airlines desk, he scowled at the blizzard outside.

"I hope we make it to the hotel," he said.

"Is it far?"

"Fortunately no, but I'd had half a mind to try to get into town. I've friends here and . . . someone I want to *see* . . ." He shrugged, a combination of irritation, frustration and worry, and then gave me a smile. "Best laid plans, huh?"

We joined the line of stranded passengers, most of whom were by now resigned. One grandmotherly type was hand-wringing over progeny waiting for her in Portland, but the clerk soothed her by saying that the airlines would phone her son and explain the case: in the meantime, here was a voucher for the hotel and she'd be called as soon as there was any change in the weather. At the moment the Rockies were in the thrall

47

of a massive cold front and blizzard conditions were covering the northwestern states.

The man directly in front of me was not so cooperative. In fact I was embarrassed by the harangue he was giving the girl about the thousands of dollars of commissions he was losing, and modern aircraft ought to be safe the way the government was throwing money and his tax dollars into research.

"Excuse me, Mac," and the man was as startled as I was by Dan's sudden interruption, "just let me get my vouchers and you can continue your tirade."

The girl clerk just stared at Dan, recovered herself and handed him two vouchers.

"See here, Mac," the salesman began, finding a new victim for his anger, "you've no idea how . . ."

"See here, Mac," Dan replied in the same ranting tone, "I think you're entirely right to blame the girl since she started the blizzard just to hold *you* up, but *I'm* tired of waiting around this place."

"The airline limousine will take you to the hotel, sir," the girl said, and then wrote out another voucher for the salesman, passing it to him with a very polite smile.

I didn't see what happened then because Dan hurried me off.

"Sorry about that, Jenny, but that sort of bastard irritates the hell out of me. Now, the baggage claim is thataway."

Our things were on the appropriately designated

carousel and mine conveniently circling as we arrived. I grabbed it off.

"My god, I didn't think a woman could travel with that little luggage!"

I awarded his comment a sour and patronizing humph and waited, tapping my foot, to see what he plucked from the moving belt. My chagrin at his modest but expensive leather case was doubled by the fact that the initials were D.J.L. What an incredible coincidence of names. I wondered what the J stood for. Maybe he was Dan-Dan, the mystery man. He was surreptitiously checking for initials on mine, but the identifying mark is the Snark Island Custom Control sticker.

"Snark Island?" he asked, perplexed.

"You haven't heard of it?" I clicked my tongue sympathetically. "Of course, it *is* very exclusive."

"Knitters only?"

He recovered quickly. He pointed towards the exit and the long profile of the hotel limousine and we made for it. As we stepped outside, the wind blasted snow into our faces. When the porter came forward to take our luggage, Dan bent to ask him something which the wind masked from me. The man shook his head emphatically and Dan shrugged, ushering me into the limousine.

"No taxis to town at all," he said, gloomy and depressed.

Our limousine was full and the driver pulled cautiously from the curb, windshield wipers going full,

but only just keeping the glass clear enough for him
to see ahead. I'd not been in Denver before and I was
not going to see much of it this trip. The drive
seemed to take longer than it probably did in objec-
tive time. No one said anything, but a soft susurrus of
sound suggested to me that the driver was swearing
under his breath. I don't blame him: even I could feel
he had little traction under the wheels. We skidded
only once going about a rotary and one of the women
in the back gave a sharp cry. I think we were all
relieved to get to the hotel entrance.

The truth came out at the reception desk when the
clerk assumed Dan and I were together and tried
putting us up in the same room.

"My name is Lovell, not Lowell," I said, enunciat-
ing clearly. "Jane Lovell."

"Sorry, miss."

I let that mistake ride because I didn't wish to get
involved with being a widow and Mrs. or Ms. or
anything, and stepped aside to let Dan have his go at
getting a room.

"You really are Lovell?" Dan asked as with several other strandees we followed a bellboy to the
elevators.

"Yes, it is rather close, Mr. Lowell."

"We'll have a drink on that. Or do you really want
to sit in your room and knit?"

"I'd love a drink." I didn't mean to put the emphasis so plainly on 'drink,' as if I were conscious of a

50

need to specify. I caught the intense look he gave me but before I could stammer an apology, he grinned.

"Or knitting needles at two paces?"

At least he didn't take offense. "I didn't know you indulged."

His humor was reflected in the mischievous glint in his eye. "As often as possible," he said, speaking through the side of his mouth.

We were in the elevator which was crowded and effectively precluded further banter.

At the ninth floor, the bellboy gestured all of us out. We were parceled off at rooms, bang, bang, bang, down the corridor. We were the last to be installed. The bellboy unlocked both doors, since they were side by side, escorting me into mine.

It was standard modern hotel, with western motif, pleasantly done: TV, large and prominent, a desk, some rather nice western and cowboy prints by Bama on the walls, the outsized bed with a striped spread. I tipped the boy and he backed out of the room with the usual patter about room service. He hadn't quite closed the door when he came back in.

"Sorry. Have to check." He fumbled with the second door on the far left. "Maid left it open after all." He used his pass key, gave me a big grin and departed.

I heard the shutting of the door in Dan's room as I made my way to the bathroom to check on my make-up.

I looked as tired as I felt and I'd half a mind to

renege on that drink. Remembering his taunt about staying in my room with my knitting, I brushed my hair, washed my hands and face, put on more mascara and lipstick, dabbed on a patch of perfume. A drink, he'd said, and the way I felt, I'd need a drink to get some sleep. I'd forgotten how dislocated one could get, time-wise, on these barnstorming trips.

There was a knock on the door.

"Look, I . . ." I started to say 'after second thoughts' . . .

"You're hungry! That's what's wrong with you. You've got to eat and this is the city for high protein, guaranteed on the hoof steak!" He grabbed my arm and had me half out the door.

"Hey, just a minute . . ."

"If you bring that knitting, I'll kill you." He hauled me forcefully into the hall.

"My key."

"Lord, and your purse if that's where your money is."

"Isn't this hotel safe?"

"I don't trust any of them these days," he said in a way that bespoke sad experience.

In the darker lighting of the hall, he looked tired, too, with deep lines from his nose to the corners of his mouth, and eyes dark with fatigue. He took my arm again, his hand warm through my wool sleeve, warm and rather comforting.

We had a drink and Dan insisted that what I needed more was the steak: I needn't have the trimmings, he said, but a decent steak would do me the world of good. So much good that he'd talked himself into having one as well. To such humorous persuasiveness it is impossible to say no. And it was very good for my morale to sip bourbon and soda in the company of an attractive man who was determined to amuse me. It was a relief not to have to wax intelligent, giving ponderous answers to self-conscious questions, or probing my unconsciousness for the 'real' reason behind some of my tales. (Funny how audiences refused to accept as a 'real' reason, the need to earn money!)

We took our drinks to the table and after we'd ordered, we both fell silent. And that, too, was unexpectedly pleasant and without strain.

"God, I'm beginning to realize how tired I am," Dan said as he stretched his long legs out under the table and arched his back against the banquette padding. "You, too?"

"Me, too." I rotated my neck against knotted muscles.

The steak was perfect: the trimmings came anyhow, comprised of baked potatoes (I do miss the Idaho in Ireland) with slathers of sour cream and butter and a green salad. The companionable silence continued as we applied ourselves to the meal. Opposite our table was a big picture window and the snow drifted idly down the pane, its progress slowed by an overhang, while beyond the leisurely flakes, the wind whipped the drifts vigorously: the effect was mesmerizing and peaceful.

A subdued babble of voices heralded the arrival of another group of snow-bound travellers but the dining room was large. The newcomers were quickly absorbed and our island of solitude preserved.

Dan ordered coffee for us and inquired after my taste in liqueurs. I hesitated and then shrugged: I'd had only the two bourbons and one liqueur was a fitting end to a good dinner. I also didn't wish to end this pleasant companionship.

The brandy was good but I would have liked an open fire, a deep couch and a chance to put my legs up.

"Trite, I know," Dan said quietly, "but I would like a roaring log fire, a comfortable couch and some decent music . . ."

"Great minds we have," and I grinned at him as I raised my brandy snifter in a toast.

"Well, they do have the roaring log fire and couches in the lounge . . ."

I thought of the crowded lounge and snorted. "That's not what I had in mind."

"Oh?" Deviltry lurked in the glint of his eyes as he leaned towards me, shifting his position so that the length of his body was against me. "What did you have in mind, my dear?" he asked in a low, suggestive tone.

"Oh, do be . . ."

"The woman's blushing. Do be . . . what?"

"Do be realistic."

"I am," he said with an exaggerated sigh. "There

is a fire in the lounge as madam wishes, and a comfortable couch, and . . .''

I caught myself before I made a blunder. He was not, obviously, propositioning me and I shouldn't assume he was for all the cliché he was rehearsing. What had almost made me betray myself was the fact that I must subconsciously have been thinking of him sexually for he was very attractive, and I'd been a long time without any relief. Simply because some 'types' had made offers didn't mean every man would.

''A crowded couch, my friend, and too many disgruntled fellow-travellers whom I'd prefer to avoid. The dinner, your good self, and the brandy,'' I raised the glass again, ''have mellowed my mood and calmed my troubled spirit, and I do not wish the enchantment to be dissipated.''

''Nor do I.'' He signaled to the waiter and gestured for two more drinks.

''No, really, this is quite enough . . .''

''I'd prefer to keep you in a mellow mood, Jenny . . .''

''I appreciate that, Dan, but I won't be much company. I'm all talked out: I'm afraid I can't rise to the occasion.''

''My dear Jenny, I'm the one who's supposed to rise.'' He delivered the line with such a straight face that it took me a moment to react. I covered my mouth to dampen my chortle of surprise. I have the most bawdy laugh at times, an embarrassment to escorts and editors who seem to assume that a children's author is necessarily humorless and obtuse.

"No, please, Dan. I'm not much of a drinker."

"What you need is a good roaring drunk, my friend, and this is the night . . ."

"Flying with a hangover is not fun . . ."

"We're flying nowhere tomorrow by the look of that weather. And one more brandy won't make you drunk but you'll sleep the better for it. And you look as if you need that."

"Thanks a lot."

"I do, too." He said it with such quiet intensity that I relented. Something was bothering him and out of sheer human courtesy, I must respond to that need. I know that I hated to drink by myself and hadn't. The least I could do was keep him company in his need.

So we had two more brandies, and then a third set. It was eleven o'clock of a fine blizzardy night when he signalled for the check. I hadn't a clue what was bothering him but I'd two new jokes that I'd have to remember to tell Mairead when I got back home. When he rose, he bowed to me, extending a hand to raise me from the banquette. I was a lot steadier than I'd thought I'd be after those brandies.

"You see, Jenny, I can judge to a nicety what you're capable of drinking."

"This once."

"Anytime. You're a good drinking companion."

We said goodnight formally at our respective doors

and I heard him snap on the night latch at the same moment I turned my own. For some reason that gave me satisfaction. But, as I undressed for bed, I was beset with the reluctant wish that he had pushed his luck with me. The real reason I don't drink much is that liquor makes me amorous. And if there's anyone at all reasonably masculine around, I get smarmy. I don't tolerate that condition in myself any more than I like it in other women. I'd gotten involved twice with unsuitable partners because of this tendency and had one helluva time disentangling myself. It would be all right if I didn't pick such lousy specimens of the male sex: men who looked for the maternal type because they were, essentially, immature and wanted a replacement mother figure. I shook my head, washed my face, brushed my teeth and climbed into bed, hoping that Dan-man had been right about four brandies putting me to sleep.

I hadn't opened the window and the snow was driven like pellets against the panes. I don't think I listened very long.

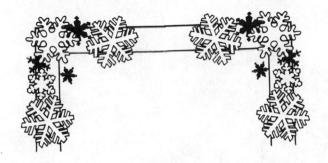

IV

"WAKEY, WAKEY, WAKEY!"

I turned over, trying to isolate the sound and identify it.

"Wakey, wakey! C'mon, Jenny, see the record blizzard blizzing."

There was a weight by my feet and someone pushing at my hip. I screwed my body around and blurrily recognized that it was Dan sitting on the edge of my bed. Just beyond him was a bellboy, angling a room-service table past Dan.

"Breakfast's served. It's ten o'clock of a miserable day. Rise and shine!"

"You are impossible!"

"Hungover?"

"No," I said after due consideration. "But if it's a miserable day, why do I have to have anything to do with it? I could sleep!"

"Ah, but too much sleep is bad for you. Here you are," he said the last to the bellboy, signing the bill and passing out the tip, "and besides, I'm awake."

"Oh, you are all heart."

"Here!" he threw my robe at me. "Get dressed!"

"I hate you," I said, feeling disheveled, face-creased and bad-mouthed. I hate to be discovered in such a state, even by my own son. I fingercombed my hair as I struggled upright and wriggled out from under the blankets. I wove slightly as I made for the bathroom. "I hate you."

"Never at our best in the morning, are we?"

I seized the first thing I could reach, the literature the hotel laid out for its guests, and flung it at him. He laughed, raising his arms to fend off the paper shower. I tried to slam the bathroom door, but the hinges were stiff and all I did was strain my arm muscles. I turned on the water hard, to cover the sound of his laughter. What gall!

I tried to avoid my image in the mirror as I wet the facecloth but I felt compelled to survey the damage. My face was, indeed, creased by the pillowslip, my eyes deeply shadowed, I'd no eyebrows on and no lipstick and I really need the color. The lines at my eyes and across my cheeks were definitely age-wrinkles, not laughter lines. About the only presentable feature was my hair, which I had had done in St. Louis. I'm only remotely a red-head: the encroaching white threads have turned my hair into a very soft, muted ginger and I keep it cropped short in curls. It's very attractive for hair. I brushed it thoroughly and flicked the curls into place. I put on eyebrows and lipstick. Then, fortified, I buttoned up my robe and went out.

He had seated himself at one of the chairs, reading a newspaper in long folds, his profile outlined against the swirling snow and grey light outside. He had a strong profile but I hadn't noticed the bump on the bridge of his nose before.

"C'mon, Jenny, your breakfast is getting cold."

"I appreciate the thought but I deplore the timing."

He eyed me critically as I approached but rose, with a grin, and held the chair for me to be seated. As I spread the napkin, (to cover the knees because gown and robe were shorties), he poured me coffee.

"You'll be pleased to know that the entire northern half of the country is socked in by this blizzard."

"Hmmmm." I took a sip of coffee, squinted at the huge glass of orange juice. "I trust this is all on the airlines," I said, toting up the room service cost against what I had with me in cash. I'd been sending money back to my Dublin bank after every engagement, keeping only enough for current expenses. I sighed.

"You bet. If big birds annoy Snowking, big birds must pay."

The orange juice was real, and I sipped appreciatively, beginning to take an interest in details. There was toast, an assortment of danish pastries, marmalade, jelly, a plateful of butter and two covered dishes at each place. I hate eggs first thing in the morning.

"Steak?" I exclaimed, peeking under the lid.

"This hyar is cow country, ma'am, best steaks in the world."

"For breakfast? This is *not* Australia." I lifted the lid higher to see if there were eggs on the meat.

"You need feeding up."

"Christ, I need a diet!"

"You're an ungrateful wench."

"I am not. Not really," I said, moderating my tone because I really did appreciate his thoughtfulness, even the steak. "It's just that I'm not a big eater, usually."

"Snacking. That's what you've been doing," he said in a carping tone, pursing his lips like an irate father. "Never eating properly; then you don't understand why you're too tired to enjoy life."

"Oh, not at breakfast . . . daddy."

He laughed and I could see where he'd nicked himself shaving, and even missed a few odd hairs on one side of his jaw. Somehow that little detail softened my attitude towards him. He folded up the paper.

"Look at it this way, Jenny. With a good steak under your belt, you don't need to mess with lunch."

"Oh, in that case . . ." and I took the lid off the steak and lifted my cutlery.

After the first bite, I began to see the solid sense of a steak for breakfast, particularly good juicy tender tasty steak.

"Feel better?" he asked when we had both finished.

"Indeed I do and I thank you and apologize for my grembling."

"Grembling?"

That's a combination of greeting and grumbling. Greeting being the Scots for moaning."

"Grembling. Very descriptive." He handed me the paper. "Not that there's much in it." He poured more coffee, draining the pot. "Shall I order more?"

I shook my head. I had an overstuffed feeling since my usual breakfast is five or six cups of coffee.

"Say, how did you get in this morning?"

His eyes danced. "You are awake now, aren't you?"

I repeated my question.

He shrugged, avoiding my eyes. "I did order breakfast for two."

"Then the bellboy . . ."

"Unlocked the door to admit your breakfast and . . . me." He wore an air of injured innocence. "You are too suspicious by far, madame. I was only doing me daily good deed."

I gave a heavy sigh. "You are gallantry itself, sir. Chivalry is not dead."

"Not as long as you keep me in my place." He cocked his head at me, that devil gleam back in his eyes. He was teasing, wasn't he?

The room phone buzzed, startling me, and him. I rose hurriedly, almost knocking the service table over, to answer the phone, feeling oddly guilty. It was the airlines, apologizing for the delay and contritely explaining that the runways were clogged with snow, making take-off or landing impossible. I would be kept advised of any changes. Did I wish them to contact anyone at Portland? No? Then I was to enjoy the facilities of the hotel.

I heard Dan moving, saw him head towards the door, gesturing at me that he was going to his room, undoubtedly to receive a similar call. I heard the muted burr of his phone and the rumble of his voice as I set about dressing. I'd even put some things in the basin to wash when the phone rang again, and it was Dan on the line.

"So, now what are we going to do with our day?" he asked.

"I don't know about you but I've . . ."

"Knitting?"

"I'll reserve that for later."

"There's a swimming pool here. Have a dip with me?"

"After that steak? I'd sink. So would you."

"In an hour?"

"Well, . . . I've no swimming suit."

"That's no big problem."

"Tank suits," I said in clear acid tones, "are great for the young . . ." thinking of the sort of emergency equipment likely to be in dressing rooms of hotels.

"You really need to work off that steak, and last night's brandy," he replied with a tolerant, patient chuckle for my evasion. "All that standing about yakatting, drinking cocktails, fending off undesirables . . ."

"That can be exercise, too . . ."

"Okay." He rang off.

It struck me that he gave up easily, or maybe I'd been too egregiously disagreeable. He was only being chivalrous. Undoubtedly time would hang heavy in a storm-struck hotel without a pleasant companion, and I had been accessible and considerably more agreeable last night.

The maid came to do the room so I went downstairs to get some stamps. This would be an ideal time to catch up on thank-you notes and answer the fan letters which had been forwarded from my publishers to St. Louis. And I'd have to tell Tim about being blizzarded. I had, after all, several times wished in his presence that I'd see some snow while I was back in the States.

The lobby was full, mostly of disgruntled travellers. While I could appreciate their positions, and supposed that if my lecture dates were being missed, I'd complain, too, I was glad enough to complete my errand and retire to my room. There was a disquieting unease in the lobby . . .

The maid was just finishing my room when I returned so I settled dutifully at the desk with my paper work. I'd brought my diary up to date, including the meeting with Dan-man, and got as far as addressing an envelope to Tim and heading his letter before I realized that I did not want to write. I stared out at the swirling snow for inspiration and found none. I was reaching for the knitting bag when I heard a knock on the door.

I was so glad to see Dan standing there that my face must have mirrored my relief. His eyebrows went up and his eyes twinkled.

"There's nobody, but nobody in that pool. They're all . . . what was your word, ah yes, . . . grembling in the lobby and the bars. The atmosphere is intense." Then he held up both hands: in one was a woman's black swimming suit and in the other, a man's green trunks. "As requested, untank-style. How's about it?" He held the suit out to me.

"How'd you know my size?"

"I asked for a fourteen?" he grimaced against my reaction.

"That should do."

He grinned with relief. "Thought so. You're not skinny, you're not fat but you have . . . ahem . . . broad shoulders. I took a chance. You're not insulted? Good. Lifeguard says we can change there but bring towels or it's another buck."

The pool was not in the basement, but at the end of one wing of the ground floor. Snow was piled against the glass surrounding the pool and lay heavy on the winter roofing. We were still the only ones taking advantage of the facility. I wondered about swimming because the pool room was chilly, with steam rising from the water.

I put an exploratory hand in the water and found it suitable.

"To your liking, madam?" asked Dan, and I was glad I was still in my clothes because I suspected he might have unceremoniously dumped me into the water if I had been changed.

"Passable, passable." I retreated with great dignity to the dressing rooms, his chuckle echoing in the empty chamber.

The fourteen fit but it was only a shade more flattering than a tank suit. There's no escaping the fact that my figure is thickening in the middle. I turned this way and that, sucking in my guts but Esther Williams I am not, even if my legs are still rather good. Ah, who cares?

I jammed a cap over my hair. Vanity! Vanity!

He was cavorting in the water, launching himself up and down, arms extended, bringing them down hard, to splash mightily, the way kids do. It was gratifying to me to notice that he was thickening about the middle, too, though with his breadth of shoulder, his spread wasn't noticeable when he was clothed. He breaststroked to the side of the pool when he saw me.

"The water's just great. C'mon in." He made a snatch at my ankle and I neatly dove over his head into the water.

It was cooler than I'd thought but warm after the outside temperature. Still, I wanted to keep moving so I began to swim a lap.

"You in condition?"

"Not for a race," I replied.

"Shall we see how many laps we can do?" He was challenging me.

"Fair enough." We'd just see.

He moderated his stroke to mine so we could swim side by side. The first couple of laps weren't too bad. Each one was progressively harder to complete: my legs got leaden, my arms, particularly my shoulders, resisted being forced to function. Then his elbow caught and shoved water right into my open mouth so I had an excuse to stop. I half-choked so that he had to tow me to the side of the pool where I could hold on until I got my wind back in the proper pipe.

"Can't we stop now?" he asked, blowing very hard through his mouth.

"I'd think we'd better." I was heaving as badly as he. "I don't think I've swum like that for years . . ."

"Me either!"

Then we both laughed together at each other.

"Ah, vanity!" he said, starting to hoist himself

out of the pool. He fell back into the water with a loud groan.

"Why do they waste youth on the young!" I hand-over-handed myself on the pool's edging to the ladder and found even that hard on my overworked arms.

I dried off and then wrapped up in the towel for the air was chill.

"I'm absolutely jacked," he said, flopping onto one of the sun loungers.

I lay down, more gracefully I thought, on the adjacent lounger. My body seemed to throb with the exercise.

"You know something, Dan?"

"What?" His eyes were closed but he turned his head in my direction.

"I'm aware I've got blood again."

"Oh?" He frowned in brief consideration. "Yeah. I have, too."

My blood was pounding through leaden limbs, my heart ought to have been audible to him from the sound of it against my rib cage. Then the inner tumult quietened and I was aware of the hiss of the snow against the glass behind me. I slewed around, trying to peer beyond the swirls. I sensed rather than saw buildings beyond, the regular bumps of parked snow-covered cars, the looming pyramids of the evergreens, their snow-burdened branches drooping.

A groan from Dan roused me and I saw him sitting up on the edge of the sun-lounger. He was flexing his shoulder muscles and stretching his arms out.

71

"Christ, am I out of condition!"

"Smoking too many cigarettes? No, you don't smoke."

"Care for another . . . slow . . . lap to loosen up?"

I groaned inadvertently as I swayed to an upright position. "Will it do any good?"

"Can't do us any more harm."

I could feel the stress in my legs and staggered to the side of the pool. I did manage a graceful dive but then, I hadn't overdone that. I couldn't swim overarm so I sort of frogged it down to the farther end. He splashed as energetically, if unscientifically, beside me. But the water was relaxing, even if all it did was hold up the muscles. We lay, flat out, flapping our hands to keep flotation, occasionally drifting together.

"This is the daftest way to spend a snow-bound morning," said Dan, a ripple of amusement in his voice.

"Isn't it?"

"By rights, we should be out there, snowshoeing, or skating or skiing. Making use of the opportunity. Lord, I haven't had the time to ski in so long."

"I haven't had the opportunity although someone started an artificial snow slope in Dublin."

"In Dublin?" He roared at the notion and I wondered if I should look hurt and defend my adopted city. "Well, we're in Denver now, and Aspen is the winter ski capital . . ."

"And I'm not up to any more exercise today!"

72

"Neither am I." He grimaced ruefully. "Know any good two-handed card games? Excluding poker!"

"Yes, as a matter of fact, I do. I picked up a three volume set of games of patience in Dublin . . ."

"I hadn't noticed the Irish were noted for their patience!"

"Don't be snide. Whatever else could the poor women do while waiting for their men to come back from whatever revolution they were fighting?"

"Match point!" He got to the ladder first but waved me up before him.

As well we had finished with the pool because a group of children and three adults plowed into the room, their noisy conversation reverberating through the empty, marble-tiled space. Dan and I locked eyes, nodded and made for our towels and respective dressing rooms. He was waiting for me when I emerged and I disliked him. His hair was neatly combed and reasonably dry. Mine was still straggly damp and I did not look my best. I was feeling chilly after all my exercise.

"You're blue in the lips."

"You've no tact, Dan. Besides, blue is the very latest fashion shade . . . see my nails?"

He gave my back a rough rubbing; to restore circulation, he told me as we made our way to the elevator.

"It's my lips is blue," I reminded him, straightening my back away from his not too gentle knuckles.

"Look, you go up to your room. I'll meet you

there. Wrap yourself in a blanket. I want to get cards.''

"I've got a pack."

"Just go along to your room, will you?" He gestured me to the elevator.

I obeyed, almost too cold to move. I had no sweaters in my suitcase: no one had predicted the damned blizzard. I knew the hotel room had felt overly warm to me after years in Irish rooms, but now it didn't seem warm at all. Swimming during a snowstorm was the daftest notion! I put my cloak on first and then the spare blanket and was still fighting the shivers. The door got knocked on.

"You squaw, me Indian brave," Dan said in the doorway. "Me got fire-water," and he displayed a fifth of bourbon and a six pack of soda.

"I thought it was cards you needed."

He jerked his chin at his shirt pocket. "Not much choice but at least I know you can't have marked the deck."

"I *never* cheat!" And then I winced at the coy floral design on the biliously colored decks.

"Pink for you, blue for me," said Dan, shoving me back into the room so he could close the door.

My comment was an unspellable sound.

He got glasses from the bathroom and splashed bourbon into one.

"Knock this back while I get the ice."

The bourbon warmed pleasantly all the way down.

I gave a convulsive shudder but immediately felt better.

"Now for a proper drink," Dan said, returning with the icebucket.

We played cards for the rest of the afternoon: Russian bank, Chinese patience, what he insisted on calling Swedish Canfield to keep the games international in flavor and educational in experience, and Brazilian canasta. It was more fun than I've had in a long while: genuine, unstrained, relaxing fun.

Abruptly I folded, what with the bourbon, the exercise and, I suppose, the residual fatigue of my trip.

"Hey, I'm winning," Dan protested.

"Hmmm. I'm sleepy." With no more apology, I crept from the chair to the bed, and curled up. I do remember that he tugged the blanket down to cover my feet.

It was hard to struggle out of the pit of sleep but I felt an obligation to do so. The mind roused more quickly than the body, however. My eyes declined the first commands to open. I was on my left side, bundled in a beautifully warm cocoon, my hands tucked under my chin, my forehead against something warm. I took note of the assorted odors, clean shirt, aftershave, male.

My eyes finally obeyed and there was a pool of light just beyond me. The warmth came from a male body.

I groaned. I hate to be seen with a sleep-creased face: it makes me look so elderly.

"Ah, the dead arose and was seen by many."

"Any is too much."

Dan chuckled and I kept my head down, hoping that he'd have the grace to turn away and let me dive to the bathroom unobserved.

"Feel rested?"

"I can't move. Go away."

"Is that gratitude for my solicitous guardianship?"

"Oh, have the natives been restless? Are we under attack from palefaces?"

"None," and laughter rippled in his voice, "these past four hours or more."

Lord, I'd never get to sleep tonight.

"What time is it?"

"Exactly . . ." I could feel him moving as he consulted his watch, "ten twenty-two, at the sound of the tone." And he hummed.

"Jaysus." I moved, but not very far: the blanket was strangling me. "What did you put on me? A strait jacket?" I punched at the restraint.

He helped me and as he loosened the blanket, looked me full in the face. I averted my head.

"What's the matter?"

"Nothing . . ." I said it sharply because my vanity was bruised and it was all very stupid of me and I knew it.

"What is the matter, Jenny?" And damn him, he got his hand on my chin and jerked my face around, his eyes searching mine.

And like a stupid fool I wanted to cry. The stupid-

ity being why did it matter how he saw me. But it
did. There's that much of the romantic left in me. Or
was I fooling myself about that, too, and all I had left
was my precious idiotic vanity?

"Your face is all creased," he said, "like a sleepy
child's." There was no distaste in his voice and he
rubbed at my left cheek as if to iron it smooth. There
was also no flattery in his observation. He couldn't
have picked a neater way to devastate me. Which is
why, when he bent to brush lips with me, the way
one does a sleepy child, the contact was charged.

"My God," he said, staring down at me with
amazement and then he kissed me again, in no way
how one kisses a sleepy child. His moustache was
soft against my lips but a couple of the bristles pricked
my nose so that I squirmed to get in a more comfortable position. His arms clamped down on me as if he
thought I was trying to evade him and his kiss became
more determined.

I couldn't recall a single kiss so emotionally charged
and I cooperated wholeheartedly. Which seemed to
encourage his efforts. And he knew how, hands and
lips, and the pressure of his body against mine.

I could have cried out in protest when he drew
away. He gave me a little shake and my eyes opened
involuntarily. His face was so close that I couldn't
distinguish his features, only the blur of the moustache,
the darkness of his eyes, the silver of his hair outlined
against the bedside light.

"Shall we, Jenny?" he asked softly.

I'd been of half a mind to try and laugh off that kiss, a major feat, but 'shall we' defeated my intention.

"Yes, please!"

He laughed, low, and if it was not a smug laugh, it had a very self-satisfied ring to it. He began to kiss and caress me again in the most leisurely, expert fashion.

"I'm trapped in the damned, blanket," I said, getting my mouth free.

He chuckled. "I know. I'll free you in my own good time."

Which he did. And freed me of some other things, too. Like my dignity, my vanity, and a few unnecessary inhibitions. By the time he had finished with me—no, by the time we had satisfied each other—because this was, above all else, a mutual effort, we both drifted off to sleep, completely relaxed.

I must have turned so that the bedside light was shining in my eyes for light woke me. I lay there, Dan's head buried on my shoulder, several other appendages draped heavily on my right side. I moved and his hand gripped me possessively as he muttered in his sleep against my shoulder.

I was hungry: I needed to go to the bathroom and the light would prevent me from going back to sleep but I couldn't reach the switch with him all over me. I didn't really want to move because it was so incredibly good to be sleeping next to a man—particularly one who did not snore. I tried to reason with my body. My stomach growled and the pressure on my bladder was something I couldn't ignore much longer in comfort.

I eased myself free of his legs, gently removed his arm and by depressing my shoulder into the pillow, managed to winkle out from under his head. I was sliding from the bed when his hand caught my arm.

"Don't go."

"I'd better or I will."

"Oh," was his sleepy groan and he flopped over.

I sped to the bathroom. Then I looked at my face which wasn't sleep-creased but very smug. I washed it in cold water to make it behave, brushed on new brows, rinsed my mouth.

"Hey, don't hog the place," he called cheerfully.

Hmm. Yes. My robe was on the door and, let's face it, at my age, things begin to sag a bit. I didn't want the magic to go because the frog-princess still looked like a frog when the kissing stopped.

Sometimes when you meet your partner after sex, there's a bit of strain. He passed me on the way to the bathroom with a broad grin on his face and a quick caress.

"Help yourself to the sandwiches but don't eat 'em all," he said just as I spotted the room service table by the window.

When had that materialized? Well, if there were to be frog princesses, there could also be djinns in the middle of storm-bound Denver.

The covered dishes exposed enough sandwiches for four—roast beef and turkey, a tasteful array of salad greens with dressing on the side, butter and rolls, two generous portions of lemon meringue pie and coffee, still reasonably steamy in its vacuum container.

I was eating with relish and speed when he joined me, dressed in shirt and trousers. Some men look sexier with an open shirt exposing their masculinely hairy chests and he was one of them.

"When did you conjure all this?" I asked with my mouth full.

"When you corked off the first time."

"Good thinking! And thanks!" I glanced at my watch. "One thirty? Whee. Very good thinking."

"Plan ahead!" He was grinning broadly and the sparkle in his eyes was infuriating.

"Plan ahead, huh?" and I waved at the rumpled bed.

"Well," and he scratched the back of his head, "it did occur to me last night . . ."

"Ergo, all the brandy?"

"Well?" And his eyes mocked me with laughter. "Should I have pushed my luck?"

It was a challenge and, because I have always prided myself on a disastrous honesty, I didn't hesitate. "You could have. But I'm glad you didn't." His hand, warm and strong, covered mine and his eyes were kinder, less wary. "This . . ." and I inclined my head towards the bed ". . . turned out rather . . ."

"Rather special. Thank you, Jenny."

We were both a trifle embarrassed by such mutual honesty and began to eat.

"I don't remember when I've been so ravenous," I said, tossing the napkin to the disarrayed table. We'd cleared it of all edibles.

"It's been a long time since your breakfast steak," he reminded me with a mildly lecherous arching of his eyebrows.

"That's very true."

A sudden rattle against the curtained windows drew me to rise and look out. I shivered, staring at the stormy night.

"I said it once too often."

"Said what?" he asked, standing behind me and parting the curtain farther.

"I said I wanted to see snow while I was in the States."

Puzzled, he looked down at me. "Aren't you American?"

"Yes, but I live in Ireland."

"Why?" He was genuinely surprised.

"Tax exemption."

"Oh, yes, you did mention you're a writer."

The wind dashed a slurry against the window and instinctively I yielded back. He caught my shoulders because I also stepped on his toes.

"Sorry."

"Not a fit night for man, beast or machine."

"Will it blow itself out by tomorrow?" I asked, sort of hoping it couldn't although perhaps it would be better if we were released from the snow thrall.

"I doubt it." He preferred that it continue. He

wrapped both arms around me and pressed me back against him, kissing the side of my neck, just where I happen to be very sensitive. "This is a real three-day howler."

"How can you be sure?"

"I grew up in Colorado. I know that note in the wind."

His hands dropped to where I was also sensitive.

"It's two o'clock in the morning and all's well. Shall we?" The last two words came out in a husky, compelling invitation, reinforced by an especially clever kiss. I nodded.

While the storm continued, so would the spell, so why not?

V

WHEN I WOKE THE NEXT MORNING, I was on my left side. The room service table was gone, but curtains pulled back. It was still blowing a fearful gale. Someone was whistling in the next room.

In the next room! I sat upright, pulling the sheet up to my bare breasts. The communicating doors were ajar.

"Why, you lousy finkface!"

"The dead arose?" He leaned around the door, a broad grin breaking through the lather on his face.

"How long have those doors been unlocked?"

The grin broadened, showing his white teeth. "Since we got here."

I remembered the bellboy's door busy-ness.

"Ohhhhh!"

"Well, plan ahead," he said with a cheerful shrug. "You don't really want to report it to the management, do you? I've only tried to preserve your reputation. All the room service came to *my* door."

I made a rude noise.

"Oh, sorry. Thought you'd approve my chivalry." He made me a bow and, considering the fact that his towel parted across his thighs, that he had a lathered razor in one hand and the aerosol can in the other, it was a noble attempt. I had to laugh.

"Look, let's swim before that family invades our pool again." He rotated his shoulders. "I need to loosen up."

If he'd asked me, I'd've been glad to vouch for his suppleness after his antics last night.

"Naughty, naughty," he said, waggling the razor at me as if my thought had been that obvious. "I'd better finish this nonsense but I won't be long. Hey, and you'd better put on the latch in case the chamber maid checks the doors and ruins our cover."

I got up, washed, made-up which was foolish since it would all come off swimming, pulled on the bathing suit and my robe, and threw the big bathtowel over my shoulder.

He was just emerging from his room as I came out. He slipped his hand under my elbow and we marched in step to the elevator, irreverently chanting 'we're off to see the wizard' under our breaths.

The pool was all ours again: the lifeguard waved to us as if pleased to have some company, then he went back to his cross-word puzzle. We did an easy fifteen laps and then floated about until we heard the unmistakable noise of childish invasion.

"You know what," he said as with mutual understanding, we got out of the water, "I feel very hungry and we're in time for lunch today."

"Hey, what about my breakfast steak?" I asked petulantly.

"No complaints. You're getting steak for lunch."

"In that case . . ."

"Tell you what—let's give 'em all a break. We'll dine downstairs."

"Are they up to us?"

"Let's give 'em a try." He glanced at his watch, which he'd just strapped back on. "Look, I've got to make a few phone calls. I'll meet you at the western room in about an hour? Okay?"

"Fine!"

"That'll give you time for a few rows of knitting. I've been keeping you from it." His eyes twinkled.

"That's only pick-up work."

"And me?"

"You ungentleman, you. *You* picked *me* up, and you know it! You . . . you . . . plan-ahead artiste!"

"An hour, then? Okay, Jenny?"

We unlocked our respective corridor doors and discreetly parted company.

The maid had been in and the room was all neat and far too impersonal, wiping out the pleasant memories of the previous night . . . and early morning. My unfinished letter to Tim was neatly centered on the desk. Evidently the hotel staff really did dust in this place. In other rooms I'd occupied briefly over the past three weeks, my things were always scrupulously left where I had put them, dust, glass-rings notwithstanding.

The red blinker on my phone was patiently flashing which meant a message. Who knew where I was? The airlines did. The message was merely to confirm what any halfwit would have guessed: all flights were grounded. I asked the operator if she'd heard a recent weather report. Her careful reply was that there was no change anticipated in the next 24 hours. She was so sorry.

"I'm not," I told her. "This is the best rest I've had in weeks."

Her tone thawed, as if she were rather relieved not to be dumped on with more complaints.

I toweled dry my hair: I'd need a set before Portland but I'd have time for that, maybe after tomorrow's swim . . . if there was one tomorrow. I completed the note to Tim, telling him about being snow-bound and blaming myself for the overdose of the fluffy white stuff. I gave him the place of the Los Angeles engagement which had only been confirmed to me in St. Louis, and reconfirmed that the Dallas and Tulsa lecture dates were unchanged. I sealed the letter and saw that I had time before meeting Dan. I laughed as I stuck the airmail stamp on Tim's letter because it was likely to reach him faster by dogsled. Ho-hum for the disadvantages of modern conveniences.

I posted the letter in the lobby box, wondering briefly if the blizzard had deflected the noble mailmen from their rounds, and then wandered towards the western room. My path took me past the boutique which announced a sale. On ski togs. Well, it was March and I had a few moments, so I went and browsed. Some of the jackets would be great protection against the chill damp of an Irish winter. The green one was not only in my size but in my budget at a third off.

"There's 40% off on some of these, miss," said the salesgirl helpfully. "Just slip it on."

I did and the jacket not only fit but the green did nice things to my hair and figure. Some greens look all wrong against my mildewed locks.

"How about matching pants?"

"I'm not a skier."

"Were you grounded, too?"

"Yes, indeed. But I'm rather enjoying it."

"You're one of the few," she said with a grimace of stretched patience.

"Sometimes people have to be forced to rest and relax: they lose the habit of taking things easy."

"You're so right." Her agreement was heartfelt.

I spotted a gorgeous sweater in almost the same tone green, but lighter, with white designs. My size and 40% off. I couldn't resist it. I was getting so bored with my travel wardrobe. And the selection in the States is much better than it is in Ireland. I told her so and she evinced a more than cursory interest that I lived in Ireland: her great grandfather had been born in Ireland but she couldn't remember where. Her idle conversation led me to buy not only the sweater and jacket but dual layer ski underwear, a heavy pair of socks and some calf-height furry mukluk type boots: guaranteed waterproof, "considering that it rains more in Ireland than it snows."

She was rummaging in the small service part of the shop for a plastic shopping sack when Dan came in.

"Bought the place out yet?"

"Some good bargains."

He had to pass the rack of ski jackets to reach me at the counter and, absently examined a sales ticket, stopping altogether to pull the jacket out of the group. It was a match to the one I'd bought.

"Mine to yours, and it's a White Stag. You're right about the bargain," he said, brandishing it. He reached to his hip. "Damn! Left my credit cards in my briefcase. Look, Jen, you go on in to the restaurant and grab us a table. The place is filling up fast. I'll be right back."

He was gone just as the girl returned with my package. It was a bit more unwieldy than I'd thought.

"I can have the bellboy take it up to your room, if you'd like."

"Would you? It's a bit much to stick under a lunch table. My name is Jane Lovell and my room is 903."

"Sure thing, Miz Lovell. It'll be there when you've finished lunch. Have a good day . . . if you can!"

"I can and will!"

Dan had been right about the restaurant being crowded. There was only one small table that I could see and the maitre d' was rushing about on the far side. I could hear other voices in the short corridor from the main lobby to the restaurant so I simply sat down at the two seater. Before I could tell the waiter who poured my water that there'd be two, he'd handed me one menu and disappeared. I was reading the description of the Grill column when I was conscious of someone standing in front of the table.

"Miss, we're extremely busy today, would you mind sharing with this gentleman?"

I was about to refuse when I looked up and saw that the maitre d' had escorted a soberfaced Dan to the table. I glanced around suspiciously as if to confirm the condition and then graciously inclined my head in permission.

"You bitch," said Dan *sotto voce*, screening his face from the next table with his menu.

"I'm only preserving the fiction you started . . ."

"I'll get you later."

"I wish you would," I said in my archest social

manner and nearly yipped out loud as he pinched my knee.

The waiter materialized, deposited bread and butter, asked which airlines and hovered with marked impatience for our orders. With just a glance at me, Dan ordered us two steaks, medium rare, baked potatoes and salads. The waiter collected the menus in one snatch and disappeared. Forever, I was beginning to think just as he finally served our long delayed luncheons.

Dan had been abstracted in the long interval between ordering and receiving. The noise and confusion in the restaurant were worse than the service, making conversation difficult. After the first three attempts to involve Dan in light conversation failed, I left him to his private reflections. His business phone calls had obviously given him problems. Fortunately the steaks were very good but with one accord, we cleared out as soon as we'd finished. I'd had my fill, certainly, of bits and snatches of other people's disgruntlements.

"Say, I bought that jacket, Jenny, and since you're equipped, let's christen 'em. Anything to leave this tower of bitching Babel." His voice was tense as he led me toward the elevators. "D'you have any warm pants with you?"

"Pants and ski underwear."

"That's great." He smiled as he spoke but retreated to his private thoughts as the elevator schwushed us up to the ninth floor.

I was admiring myself in the mirror when he tapped on the connecting doors. I fumbled, remembered I'd locked it, undid the catch and opened it to gasp in startlement. The apparition in the black, green and white ski mask fortunately spoke in Dan's voice. He dangled another ski mask from his hand.

"You'll need this. It's goddamned cold outside. And these," and he offered me thick insulated mittens as well.

I had trouble fitting the eyeholes and nose place until he gave the knitted helmet an expert twitch.

"Jaysus, it does nothing for me, does it?" I said to my circus self.

"Think of the frostbite it'll prevent and stuff your vanity."

He was irked, but not with me, so I felt it wiser to ignore his mood. We left through the side entrance rather than traverse the packed lobby. The wind lashed at us, glad of new victims and, despite my face mask, I involuntarily closed my eyes against the bite of the cold and spun snow.

"Where do we go from here?" I asked in a bellow over the wind.

"Walk!" And he indicated a general direction past the snow-covered mounds of parked cars.

In the murky distance you could make out the brighter lights of the airport buildings and the straight lines of sodium lighting. I heard the muted groan of a snowplow but it took me a long while to locate the slowly moving monster.

Dan tapped my shoulder and motioned left. I plodded beside him. Out of my mind, to be sure, but why not? It was sort of wild and eerie to be the only ones out in the blizzard.

I've no idea how long we walked; certainly we made no records for either speed or distance. The hotel sign got small and dim. I got tired so I flopped down in the snow and made an angel while Dan watched. He hauled me up and carted me away so we could admire the unmarred angel form. Then we tried to build a fort but the snow was powdery and didn't pack well. I was disappointed. Dan was, too. My face guard kept slipping and I'd end up with a mouthful of wet wool as I struggled after him. It was rather too cold to open your mouth to talk but it was my legs which gave out first. The ski underwear and the jacket lived up to the manufacturer's claims. I was, if anything, too warm between the insulation and the exercise. I sure wasn't used to walking in snow, or having to drag my feet through drifts and plunging to get out of them. I was dropping further and further behind Dan and then I just slid down a drift and let the snow hold me up.

"Dan. Dan! DAAAAAANNN."

I thought he'd just keep on walking and I got a little twinge of fear. The hotel sign was a long blur away. How could he be that thoughtless?

"DAAAAAN!"

To my intense gratification, his figure stopped, turned this and that way and then swung around.

"Hey, I'm here. Over here!" I was waving my arms to little effect so I crawled out of the drift, wigwagging more furiously until he spotted me.

"What the hell is this about?" he demanded angrily, hoisting me to my feet. "You could get lost."

"No, just tired."

"Tired?"

"We've been slogging for hours."

"Nonsense . . . it's only . . . God, you're right. It's nearly five. Goddamn, Jenny, I'm sorry. I've no right to snap at you."

"No, you haven't," I said rather equitably because we were now heading back towards the hotel. "But you've got something on your mind and I'm the only available goat."

"You're not a goat."

"Something's got yours." I let my inflection remain up, in case he wanted to talk.

He brushed the snow from me and threw an arm around my shoulders as I staggered a little.

"I've done all the talking I can, Jenny, but you've done a lot to help me."

The mouth slit in his face mask was filled with teeth, a truly horrific sight. "Let's not talk of problems, Jenny. Let's just . . . walk, huh?"

I shrugged acquiescence and he squeezed my shoulder appreciatively. The wet rim of my mask was beginning to chafe my lips so we didn't do any more talking, but a lot of grunting, as we slogged through the snow. The heat of the foyer only emphasized how

95

cold it had been outside. I felt numb on the surface. I snatched off the chafing face mask and unzipped my jacket to let the warmth penetrate.

"Dan, I want to make an appointment for my hair," I said, pointing to the beauty salon sign.

"Find me in the bar. I'll order hot toddies. We'll need them."

So we parted. My thighs were muscleless as I made my way down the steps to the salon level. Wow, was I out of condition! Would I last to the toddy, I wondered, grinning at my frailties. Not that I would have changed one moment of the past few days.

Unexpectedly the beauty salon was crowded: indoor types, I guessed. The girl who took my appointment for noon the next day kept glancing at the snow I was dripping on the modern design carpeting. Well, I expect she wouldn't be the only one to think me mad for romping in the snow like a child.

When I got to the bar, I saw Dan talking to a big man, a grossly big man who had some inches over Dan's six feet and was much broader in beam, chest and waist. He wore a stetson, pushed back on his head and a sheepskin jacket, high wellingtons. He was also the type of hearty back-thumping loud-laughing oaf that I detest and he was going through those motions with Dan. I did not wish to be exposed to that sort of character so, instead of approaching Dan, I edged round until I could catch his eye and signal him that I'd go on upstairs and leave him to his friend.

This man made Dan wary: he stood there with hooded eyes, his shoulders angled forward as if to protect . . . his back, probably, because old Hearty gave him a clomp across the shoulders that made him wince and rock on his feet. Dan caught sight of me then and with a quick shake of his head and a jerk, indicated that I should go upstairs.

Relieved, I made my way out of the crowded bar. The calves of my legs were aching by the time I got to my room so that I decided to take a bath, as hot as the water would come out of the taps. I soaked and soaked. I'd used muscles today, in the spirit of the exercise, that hadn't been called on for years. I couldn't recall the last bad blizzard we'd had while I was still in Massachusetts.

It was rather nice to be alone, too. I told myself that as an insurance buffer. I tried to mean it. Furthermore, I would not sit around in my room waiting for Dan to shake free of old Hearty. I'd noticed a snack-bar/coffee shop place by the side entrance. I wasn't hungry for a big meal or the frustration of bad service.

The coffee shop was not well patronized and the waitress absently rattled off the numerous items they could no longer supply from the menu. I was quite pleased to settle for thick bean soup and a grilled cheese sandwich. I also ordered some roast beef and ham sandwiches to take back to my room.

And who was waiting for the elevator when I got

there but Dan. With old Hearty beating him soundly about the head and ears in farewell.

"You could always bring the young lady with you, Jerry," he said. "Fran and I wouldn't mind a bit."

"I know your parties of old, Fred, but if there's any chance the weather'll clear, I've got to leave tomorrow. Take it easy on the way home, will you? Thanks again for the drinks."

Dan was so eager to get on the elevator he damned near ran down the people getting off.

"You better take it easy, too, Jerry!" said Fred with a boisterous guffaw. "You better slow down! You'll live longer that way."

I moved into the car, ignoring Dan who was ignoring me. We could both hear the hearty chuckle as the heavy door shut. Dan winced, relaxing as the elevator whisked the two of us up to the ninth floor.

"Maybe I shouldn't have refused the invitation, Jen. He doesn't live that far away. Came over in his Land-Rover. His wife's a good person and it would have been nicer for you than dossing about in this hotel."

"Me?" I'd been thinking he was only explaining why he hadn't gone with Hearty.

"You're the only lady I know here. Of course, I'd've brought you with me."

"I don't think I'd've gone, Dan. His old hearty-har-har type of host is the lowest on my list. He's a loud-mouth, back-thumping, hard-nosed bigot and if he'd done the shoulder-slapping bit with me, he'd've got a frostbitten hand.''

"He wouldn't have slapped your shoulder . . .''

"No, he wouldn't've. He'd've slipped an arm about my waist as soon as possible and done the squeeze bit, inching his hand up higher and higher till he squeezed something that'd get him a slap in the face or an elbow in that beer gut of his. He's just the sort that gets you away from the other guests, alone in a room and tries to slobber you with kisses.''

I was wound up and didn't stop until I jammed the key into my doorlock. Dan had gone from amazed to surprised amusement to outright laughter.

"I don't think you like Fred,'' he said, completely straightfaced, as he unlocked his door.

"You might indeed suspect that. Though I've never really met the man and I could be wrong.'' I had entered my room, closed the hall door, and opened our connecting doors as I spoke so that Dan lost nothing of my comments.

"You aren't,'' he said, leaning against the door jamb. "He's an underhanded, snide-cracking, double-dealing fool because he isn't subtle enough to keep from being caught out. Used to be a sheriff till he got caught taking a bribe.'' Dan brushed fingers through his hair as if to rid himself of old Hearty. "I need a drink. A peaceful drink. Join me?'' He reached for the bottle, splashing bourbon in the two glasses. "Damn! You didn't get your hot toddy!''

I laid my hand on his arm, reassuringly, and our

eyes met. His were angry, an anger that was reflected in the set of his mouth and jaw: a deep anger, not just concerned with having to put up with the society of an unwelcome character. He was disturbed and uncertain.

"The least of my worries. I had lovely hot soup in the coffee shop. I'm not much of a drinker, though I'll certainly join you and it's my turn to get the ice."

He was nursing his drink in the chair by the window when I got back. I put ice and soda in mine, added them to his and sat down in the other chair. He wasn't brooding: he was thinking, hard and deep and his ruminations were no longer uncertain. I felt he had made some decision in that short time I'd been out of the room.

"Well, there's nothing I can do about it tonight," he said with a long sigh. "Or do you approve of avoiding issues?"

"Depends on the issue, I think. Would an impartial second opinion help? I'm not prying."

"I know," and he gripped my hand tightly for a moment. "Your very good health, Jenny!"

Which is a tactful way to change a subject. So I raised my glass and drank his good health. He was evidently determined to put his problem firmly out of his mind because now he stretched out his long legs and settled himself, turning with a slight smile to ask if I'd recovered from the hike.

"After a hot bath to unknot those muscles I didn't remember having, yes. Between swimming the Hellespont and rediscovering Little America, I've racked up a rare quota of exercise for a snow-bound soul. But I needed it."

"No exercise in podium-pounding?"

"Just stamina."

"Tell me, do you enjoy that sort of thing?"

"Yes, in smaller doses. This is the first time I'd had an extended tour."

"How many engagements?"

"Twenty-five. I've done twelve. I've got Portland, four in San Francisco plus Easter off, then Los Angeles, Houston, Dallas and Tulsa."

"So far so good. You appear relatively unscathed."

"I don't know about that," I said with considerable feeling. "I was a bit scathed when I got on that plane in Milwaukee."

"Isn't that why you knit? The ravelled sleeve of care? What's that a quote from?"

I groaned. "Shakespeare, Macbeth, Act II. Scene 2, but you've used it in the wrong context."

"Good God!"

"The rewards of a literary education."

He clicked his tongue at my haughty tone. "Lo, the poor engineer!" As emphasis to his self-deprecation, the snow slashed at the window. He sat upright, glancing at his watch. "The news! May I?" He was already turning on the TV set.

We got the tail end of the 7:00 news, including the weather analysis which was bad. The country was blanketed in snow down to the Texas panhandle with

101

Louisiana, Mississippi and Alabama fighting the lowest temperatures in years. Satellite observation indicated that clearer weather was slowly moving eastward from the Pacific and we could expect the storm to blow itself out within the next thirty-six hours.

"Great!" Dan brought his hands down hard on his knees. I wasn't sure if he was being facetious or pleased. His expression gave me no clue. His actions did. He poured himself another hefty drink with only an excuse of a splash of soda.

The announcer began extolling the praises of the feature film.

"Gunga Din!"

Dan regarded me with surprise. "You want to see it?"

"I haven't seen it in years, but I met Douglas Fairbanks once in London and he's such a charming man. He must be in his sixties but he's got charisma or . . . I guess you'd call it . . . a very cultured animal magnetism because he couldn't have been nicer. My agent knew him and he came over to our table . . . we were lunching in London at a marvellous place in Jermyn Street . . . What's the matter?"

"I was just watching the way your face lights up. No, don't close down. It's a relief to see someone unafraid of showing enthusiasm."

"Even about another man?"

"He's some man. My idol as a boy!" Dan's expression was brighter, too. "Swashbuckling derring-do," and he cut an intricate swath in the air with imaginary sword.

"Well, he's every bit as glamourous as he was cast. And *not* stuffy or unpleasant. He told us he'd been in New York recently and a cabby had recognized him. Only . . ."

"Only what . . . ?"

"The cabby said, 'I saw your son on TV last night in the Corsican Brothers . . .' "

"Good God . . ." Dan roared with laughter.

"And the cabby said, 'the kid's doing great.' So Mr. Fairbanks replied that, yes, he thought the boy had a good future."

Dan chuckled over that encounter as the credits for *Gunga Din* rolled past the Indian border.

"D'you mind?" he asked, indicating he intended to stretch out on the bed to watch the movie. I didn't mind. "Then bring your knitting and join me. Best seat in the house."

My father used to say that you had to see a man drunk to judge his character accurately. I prefer men driven to drink who don't feel obliged to test their capacity in the crisis. The old film was a godsend because Dan got so involved in it, as did I, with assorted reminiscences of our childhoods, that he was just taking the last of his double jolt when Cary Grant, slung over the shoulder of Victor McLaughlin, was hauled off to the jail, brandishing a bottle of Scotch.

"Can I freshen your drink, Jenny?" Dan asked during the next commercial.

"I wouldn't mind."

Surreptitiously I watched him splash reasonable amounts. Whatever had been riding him before seemed to have eased.

"How's the knitting going?"

I spread it out for him and he smoothed down the pattern but his eyes were on my face. He bent forward and kissed me gently.

"You've a soothing effect, Jenny, and I'm grateful." He settled against the headboard as the last commercial ended and the screen faded into the movie again.

In the end, when the face of Sam Jaffe came up over the final battle scene and the sonorous lines of the poem, "You're a better man than I am, Gunga Din . . ." faded into the final credits, I had a lump in my throat and a suspicious wetness in my eyes which I hastily brushed away.

"Don't, Jenny. It's an honest response."

"I know, but . . . habit, I suppose. Tim, my son, used to get very upset when he saw me crying."

"Did he have many occasions? You don't strike me as a weepy sort."

"No, I'm not. Raymond, my husband, died of cancer of the lungs. Slowly. We knew it was hopeless. The doctor kept telling me that tears are nature's escape valve but Timmy was only five, a bit young to understand tears were therapeutic . . ."

" 'The gentle rain, that droppeth . . .' No, that's wrong, too, isn't it."

I used his malapropism as an excuse to laugh off the imminent tears of memories. "Indeed it is. That's Portia talking about mercy, not weeping jags . . ."

"Okay, which act and scene, quickly now for $100."

"Act IV, Scene 1, where's my hundred?" I held my hand out.

"Not so fast, lady. I have to check your answer." And he reached in the drawer for Gideon's Bible which made me laugh harder.

"No, not in that. Shakespeare, not Solomon. Don't you trust me?"

"Who trusts women nowadays with bra burners and petitions and all?" There was a mighty sharp edge to his voice and I know it stopped my laughter. He was immediately contrite, clasping my still outstretched hand in both his. "No, I trust *you*, Jenny. Yes, by God, I do!" He kissed my hand, first on the back and then, turning it over, in the palm in such a lovely fashion that it awoke an instant response in me. " 'There's a time and tide in the affairs of man . . .' " His wry smile and the faint emphasis on 'affairs' made me chuckle.

"You're incorrigible and grossly incorrect . . ."

"As usual. Shut up and kiss me, woman!"

I did, since I had no option, being crushed against him in a fashion reminiscent of the swashbuckling antics of Douglas Fairbanks as a Corsican brother. I don't honestly think he intended to make love to me

105

then: he was still distracted by his encounter with old Hearty. And I wasn't randy after last night.

The moment he began kissing me, I kissed him back and the contact was as charged as it had been the previous evening. He broke off, searching my face but he was too close for me to see anything except the intense gleam in his eyes.

"I'm being greedy, Jenny, but Christ, do I need you! May I?"

"Of course."

Many years before, when Ray and I were first married, I had read an article by a committee of Quakers on extramarital sex. They had decided that it could be morally wrong to deny a man the solace of intercourse, which, in their estimation, was as much a necessity to man, and woman, as water, food and shelter. They by no means condoned promiscuity or seduction but, between consenting adults, extramarital sex was permissible.

Dan-man needed me as a woman. And I rejoiced that he used me and experienced relief, gripping my arms so tightly in his climax that I suspected I'd have bruises by morning. He collapsed against me suddenly and by the evenness of his breathing, I knew he was asleep. I consoled myself with the rationalization that I had done my duty as woman all too thoroughly. I was bloody wide-awake with some 200 pounds of immovable man squooshing me into the mattress. We hadn't turned off the TV so I watched a second showing of Gunga Din, the late news which added horror tales to the earlier version of people stranded in cars in snow drifts, of houses without food, water, electricity, special patrols snow-shoeing to the rescue and scenes of snow-drifted deserted city streets and facilities, like the Denver airport. Baby, it was cold outside!

The announcer was just giving me the glad word about the late show, a trite situation comedy from the frothy pre-war years, when Dan stirred, rolled off me and flopped on his right side, arms dangling over the edge of thc bed. I slipped out, turned off the TV, got to the bathroom, put on my nightgown, got back into bed, turned off the lights and hoped that I, too, could fall asleep, my virtues being my reward.

I think it was the snow pelting the windows which soothed me to rest. It wasn't my thoughts or my unslaked emotions.

VI

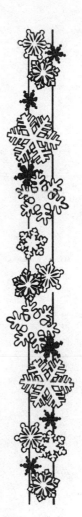

I WASN'T SO DEEPLY ASLEEP that I didn't feel Dan move: he tried to be considerate and if I'd been really down for the count, I wouldn't have roused.

"Go back to sleep, Jenny," he said, patting my shoulder gently.

"There's roast beef sandwiches on the desk," I said in a mumble.

"How'd you know I'd be hungry?"

"Page from your book. Plan ahead!" I flipped over and saw him pulling on his pants in the dark room. He moved to the desk.

"You're a doll. Want one?"

"I wouldn't mind. And there might be coffee in the machines by the ice-maker."

"By God, there might. Want some?"

"Hmmmm." I was hungry too, and blessed by plan-aheadability, though I hadn't envisioned a snack at whatever ungodly hour this was. He slipped out the door and the light from the corridor was enough to illuminate my watch dial. Four-thirty? Oh, well. He was back with two containers of coffee.

"It's black. They've run out of sugar and cream. But the night watchman told me there isn't even coffee on some of the floors."

"Good Lord and the hotel's chockablock."

"I gather a convoy will make it to our relief in the morning . . . this morning."

"Ah, fair enough!"

We finished our snack companionably in the dark. He disposed of the sandwich wrappings and the containers, undressed and got back under the covers. He turned to me, pulling me close to him, settling me beside him. I was quite willing that he go back to sleep and therefore was pleased when his free hand began to explore my body gently, rousing responses I thought dampened.

"Your turn now, Jenny," he said, his voice rippling with amusement and he held me closer when I started to protest. "Turnabout's fair play, woman, and you're so damned responsive, it's a pleasure. Now relax and enjoy. This rape is inevitable!"

I obeyed and enjoyed it far more than I had reason to think I could or would. Or should.

After Raymond died, at first I had neither the time, inclination or opportunity to play around. Then I'd had a summer love affair with a graduate student when I was studying for my dotoral thesis but it was only a summer fling. I'd had two entanglements of some duration and once thought of remarrying but time had proved the wisdom in my hesitation. I'd learned an important lesson: it takes time to become lovers, to adapt to the requirements of another man, to forget instinctive responses learned in another bed. It amazed me that there was so little adjustment to make with Dan: he was unlike any previous lover, yet we fit. Chemistry, I suppose, and the rightness of timing and the fitness of opportunity. There was no impediment to my enjoyment of this brief encounter.

I woke the next morning about ten o'clock, completely refreshed, with a terrific sense of well-being. The space beside me was empty but I heard splashings through the partly closed connecting doors. I got up, washed and pondered getting directly into my bathing suit. I'd the hair appointment at 12 but the swimming had been such a pleasure . . .

"Hey, don't dress, Jenny. Ah, you didn't," Dan said, peering around his bathroom door.

"Damn right. I want my swim."

"Then your steak. The supply wagon got through the pass at down," he added in a cowboy twang.

113

"And I think," he said in a normal voice, "the snow is beginning to let up. The wind is down."

I glanced at the window and saw the lazy fall of flakes. Regret was uppermost in my mind but a twitch of urgency nagged. I did have that evening roundtable discussion in Portland tomorrow and since this was my first lecture for them, come hell, highwater and drifting snow, I wanted to make the date on time.

We had our swim in the empty pool. I did twenty laps before I started puffing in earnest and held on to the side of the pool while Dan did three more, pleased with himself when he came to rest beside me, breathing deeply but without strain.

"I must try to swim more often," he said. "Most hotels have pools the world round."

"You travel a lot?"

"Too much."

We heard the sudden explosion of children into the pool foyer and on cue hauled ourselves out.

"Steak next, Jenny."

"I've got to get my hair done, first, please?"

"Good, then I'll do my business now. When'll you be finished?"

"Say, one-thirty."

"One-thirty in the steak room!"

A neatly coiffed head is an ego boost, a shield against the outrages of fortune and competition, as a variety of psychological aid. I had made that appointment initially for publicity purposes: now it was far more important to me to look my best for Dan.

I was finished earlier than I'd anticipated so I hurried back to my room to change into the less casual grey slacksuit. The red message light was glowing in the room. And the airlines, damn 'em, were happy to inform me that I could continue my interrupted flight to Portland at 3:40.

When I replaced the receiver, more than the red light went out. I sat staring at the goddamned thing, wishing I hadn't come back to the room, willing the blizzard to give one last gasp at keeping me in Denver. I don't know how long I sat there until I woke to the fact that I would be late for my lunch. And that would now be all I'd have of this so pleasant, so unexpected, so damned brief an encounter.

"Well, you twit, it was bloody more than you thought you'd have."

I dressed quickly but without any anticipatory exhilaration. I did my face carefully, shielding myself and my tender sensibilities behind a cosmetic mask.

"What time's your flight, Jenny?" he asked, as he stood aside to let me take the inner banquette seat.

So much for my bright smile and insouciance.

"Three-forty."

He glanced at his watch. "Let's enjoy our steaks." His hand grasped mine firmly under the table and I looked directly into his face.

I told myself first that while his mouth was smiling, there did seem to be a hint of regret in his eyes: no

115

sign of twinkle, no diffidence. The pressure of his hand reaffirmed that he, too, found the ending a bit too abrupt.

"I like the way they did your hair; it's becoming," he said and glanced down at my suit. "Good English flannel?"

"I think so, but an Irish tailor."

His raised eyebrows expressed surprise at such style.

"We're fairly cosmopolitan in Dublin, you know. Not all culchies."

"Culchies?"

"Hicks."

"Oh!"

We made desultory conversation until the waiter came for our orders. I had to approve Dan's lead, to talk of everyday inconsequentialities. The magic was trickling back into the djinn's bottle, along with the end of season blizzard. Each of us had to go back to being what we really were, instead of what we had briefly been: lovers. *Sic transit!*

The steaks were good and our conversation righted itself, wondering whether these steaks were the last in the hotel freezer or the first of the newly delivered. I wanted the lunch to go on forever so I insisted on lemon meringue pie and coffee. I almost burned my mouth trying to drink the coffee hot because I needed the privacy of my room to recover from painful things, like Dan's presence.

"Have you packed?" Dan asked, as if he too felt the same ambiguous pulls.

"No, I haven't," I said, blotting my lips, nervously anxious to leave, desperate to hold him by me.

"There's time enough, don't worry," he said, with a shadow of his wry grin. He caught my hand, not letting me go. "My flight's at 4. I'll come with you."

The lump in my throat was so ruddy big that I couldn't have said anything, even if I had had a wit left, on that eternally short elevator ascent. There were others in the car, all chattering about leaving and moaning about those who'd been waiting to meet them at various airports. We were, again, what we actually were, strangers in transit, up and down now, instead of east and west.

As we strode along the corridor to our rooms, we still said nothing. I could have wished he'd hold my hand but I was glad he didn't. He grinned at me as we went through the business of unlocking our doors. His closed the same instant mine did and I leaned against it, eyes on the connecting door, no longer ajar.

I told myself to get together, took a deep breath and began to pack. I threw in a lot of the hotel's dividends, matchbooks, wrapped soap, packaged shower caps, stationery, postcards, the room service menu—*mementi memoriae*. I fanned out the pink deck of cards nostalgically and then tucked it carefully into my handbag. I closed the case, arranged my cloak on the bed and then checked the bathroom and all the drawers as well as the closet in case I had overlooked anything.

I threw my cloak loosely over my shoulders, hefted my case in one hand, purse and knitting bag in the other, attaché case under my arm and without a sentimental backward look, opened the hall door.

"Need a bellhop, miss?" He was there, propping up the door frame, one eyebrow cocked and a humorous grin on his face.

Thank God! If he'd shown any other facet of his personality, I'd have turned soupy.

"I really must commend the manager on the alertness of his staff."

The trip down in the elevator was considerably less traumatic: my upper lip had stiffened. In the lobby, I turned towards the desk to settle whatever there was on the bill.

"Transport's this way," Dan said, inclining his head to our right. I could see one of those elongated airport limousines at the entrance.

"My bill?"

"That's all on the airlines."

"All of it?" I thought of the room service.

"I checked." He sounded so positive that I let the matter ride. "And if you volunteer to pay the room service you can find another bellhop."

I demurred and he hurried me out to the limousine. We sat companionably close, even our legs touching during the short drive to the terminal. The snowplows must have done yeoman service to open two narrow passages on the four lane roads but the snow had dwindled to gentle flakings so that the whole snow-bound panorama was visible. Denver had really been dumped on.

"You're flying United to Portland?" he asked, as we threaded our way into the main lobby. "This way."

He dropped my case at the appropriate window and then gestured that he was going to the Delta slot.

My ticket was validated and I was told that I'd be boarding in ten minutes at Gate 5. As I turned away from the counter, Dan joined me. He had two ticket folders in his hand but I didn't think much about it then.

"You don't leave until 4?" I asked to ease the constraint between us.

He shook his head, peering past me towards the busy entrance and then up at the clock. "Which gate?"

"Five."

"I'll see you there," and with a touch of his usual fun, "and vouch that we didn't spend the blizzard making knitting needle bombs."

"We were more practical than that!"

Our eyes caught and we laughed.

"Make love, not war!"

"Hallelujah . . ."

"Amen, brother."

That was just the right note to take as we strolled towards the security check, our arms linked. We paused before the security arch, to let others through. I felt suddenly awkward, impatient, restless and I turned to

119

Dan. My smile faded because he wasn't wearing one. He took my hand in both his, caressing it. He wasn't looking at me, but at my hand.

"Jenny . . ." His name for me came out in a rush. "Jenny, don't drop any stitches!" He gave my hand a fierce pressure before he turned and walked quickly away, without a backward look. Me? I almost collided with the security arch, trying to get through it. I don't remember boarding the plane. I was sitting, looking dumbly out the window at the occasional snow flakes when my seatmate nudged me to put on my safety belt. I thanked the man and belted up, trying not to look out the window at snowbound Denver.

Above the clouds at something like 37,000 feet (I remembered the captain announced the height), the sun was achingly brilliant after three days of storm greyness. Our flying time to Portland was two hours and some minutes.

To try and pin conscious thought on some occupation, I took out my diary, to bring it up to date.

I did so, reducing to spare entries of time, place and activity the most romantic interlude of my 47 years. "Hike with DJL; very cold, hard to walk far or long. Quiet dinner with DJL" "Swim/DJL: hair appointment, 12. Lunch DJL 1:30": just as if he had been any professional contact or business friend.

VII

PORTLAND WAS BROWN. After four years in Ireland, I had forgotten how brown grass becomes in winter in the northern half of the States. It is depressing: more depressing than the somewhat grey 'soft' winter days of Ireland for there the grass, being green, has a brilliance all its own, as if recalling the warmth of the sun in the grey weather. I'd prefer Ireland at its green dreariest, to the States in brown winter death.

The Portland airport was compact and new, alongside the Columbia River. The view of Mount Hood

123

and the Three Sisters as we banked to land was spectacular enough to bring me out of my temporary mental funk. Organizing myself and getting to the motel completed the process. The motel was mock Far Eastern Japanesy type, dark wood, monolithic style, and full. However, it was modern, convenient, comfortable and reassuringly anonymous. I had a drink with my dinner of Pacific crab which were much sharper in taste than East Coast shellfish. I sat and watched the river swirling in the change of tide—idling in body and mind. I took a couple of sleeping pills and conked out for a night of non-tossing and not much rest.

Taking myself firmly in hand again the next morning, I phoned Mr. Porter at Portland State University. He was delighted to hear that I had emerged from the blizzard-bound Midwest. They had seriously wondered whether I'd make the engagement. I affected surprise that they could doubt my ability to overcome a minor obstacle. I was scheduled to do a lecture, two roundtable discussions on writing for young adults, and to address a group of city librarians on the changing styles in children's reading. The only thing that had really changed was the availability of what children prefer to read rather than what adults think they should be reading, to improve their little minds. I happened to write what they wanted to read: fantastical adventures with (to adults) incredible creatures with magical powers.

Often, as I addressed my skeptical adult audiences,

I wondered if they had had any childhoods at all; they didn't seem to have enjoyed them. Probably not. If they'd been old enough to have lived through the depression, their childhoods must have been bleak. Young enough to have lived through the Second World War, they'd have another set of influences to drive them.

My editors had remarked that my ability to 'think' as a child, a contemporary child, was what made my books so popular. Perhaps. I gave full marks to my son, Timothy. After all, it had been Tim, telling *me* stories at his bedtime (his earliest tales stemming from a subconscious realization that his father was dying) which had started me on my career. Critics and child psychologists might suggest different rationales but I was *there*. And I diverted my anguish over Raymond's lingering death into jotting down Timmy's delightful bedtime yarns. Ray had enjoyed them, too, because I got into the habit of taping them rather than lose some of Tim's quaint phrasing in the retelling.

Tim has always been a demonstrative and affectionate boy but, at five, his sensitivity had told him that mother needed more than kisses and hugs: she needed to be diverted and consoled. So *he* had told *me* bedtime yarns to supply that need.

Now my empathic, sympathetic, sensitive son wants to build bridges and space ships. I'm surprised who shouldn't be: Tim is never predictable.

Nor, because of Tim, was my life. There was so little money left after Raymond died that I went back to teaching to support us. I was not temperamentally suited to that profession even after getting a Masters in Education. So, I compromised with a job in the university library where I could work hours to suit Tim's school schedule. One of the researchers gave me the right advice: get an advanced degree in library sciences and write my own ticket with any of the major industries who desperately needed properly catalogued and managed libraries. I went one better: I got my doctorate in library sciences, borrowing enough money from both Ray's and my own parents to finance the studies. It was a grind, but when I finished, I really did write my own ticket—with an aerospace firm in Cambridge.

Then, after years of working every spare minute, I was restless with the lonely evening hours on my hands. That's when I rediscovered the tapes of Tim's terrible tales to mother mom. They had lost none of their charm and, to fill in spare time, I typed them up. I showed them, more as a joke, to a friend. She asked permission to show them to her husband who was an editor in a textbook firm. The second publisher we submitted them to signed me to a contract and it was full steam ahead.

At that point in time, Timmy was in junior high school in a very rough neighborhood. With no effort on his part at all, he was getting straight A's, bored stiff and, with the exception of one very studious narrow-minded boy, friendless. Tim'd been in too many fights and when he got his skull fractured in a science lab (I never did find out the details), I realized that either we'd have to move from this town or Tim would have to go to a private boarding school. My editor mentioned the tax exemption for authors in Ireland and when I'd learned a bit more about the quality of Irish schools and life, I decided the gamble would be worth it. I'd enough savings and with continued effort at the typewriter on my part, plus a tax exemption, we could swing it.

We did. Tim was extremely happy in the Irish school system, made a quartet of good friends who were constantly in each others' pockets, did well on his Irish exams and his American college boards and SATs.

This was my second lecture tour: more extensive and better planned than the previous one. I should have a nice addition to my capital: enough to spend some time writing an adult book I'd in mind, and for Tim to stop worrying about how we were going to meet his college fees.

Mr. Porter said that he would collect me at the motel, to be sure he could deliver the speaker on time when they thought her snowbound. I was ready for him when he entered the lobby. Score one for me, I thought from his pleased expression. There's always a bit of awkwardness, when the shepherd/watchdog/p.r. man encounters Visiting Celebrity. For starters, the p.r. man has to gauge the V.C.'s egocentricity or absentmindedness. The gal who did p.r. at Milwaukee said she dreaded the absentminded darlings: the egos were much easier to handle: all you had to do was get them to talk about themselves and they'd go on for hours.

Mr. Porter started on the subject of the blizzard and that took us through the initial sparring. It amused me to wonder what Mr. Porter . . . Jim, I should say for he invited me to use his first name by the time we got to the elevated road spaghetti about Portland . . . what Jim would have said if he'd known how I actually had spent my time in Denver. Then he acquainted me with the size of my probable audiences and what aspects of writing, and library work I was expected to discuss. He'd like me to give an interview to the University radio, and one for the local newspaper. I agreed since I felt that I'd been a bit overpriced by the lecture bureau and was determined to give value for money.

The lecture went well: the hall had good acoustics, being an amphitheatre type lecture room so I didn't have to shout to be heard. The second roundtable was trying. A young girl wanted to know if any of my tales were drug-induced, which I denied categorically. She then questioned me about my private opinions of current drug restrictions and what was the climate in Ireland as regards drug-addiction.

"The climate in Ireland is always damp, and people take aspirins just as they do here."

Her indignant reply "That isn't what I mean" was drowned in the laughter and I saw Mr. Porter tapping her shoulder and speaking to her.

Last year I'd been heckled and had made the mistake of answering honestly and fully, thinking that the best policy. It had embroiled me in a rather disgusting word-brawl with the young man. Afterwards, in the bar where I'd been taken to recover by a considerate faculty member, it was pointed out to me how to handle such exigencies. If possible, you make a funny; you never explain your position unless it is germane to your lecture topic; you keep your cool and if the situation looks like getting out of hand, then you agree to discuss the matter with the heckler privately after the lecture—and conveniently forget to arrive.

I enjoyed the librarians' meeting the following morning: they were a keen bunch, and seemed familiar with my thesis on collection cataloguing and data retrieval. I noticed some faces familiar from the other lectures and wondered if the students had misunderstood the topic. Or, maybe they were indeed library science students. I got sidetracked onto children's books in Ireland toward the end of the meeting but I honestly feel that the British Isles have marvellous children's books, inexpensive, well-produced and with understated content. You don't have to bludgeon facts into children's minds: they're a lot more perceptive than most adults will credit them; and 'perceive' is the operative word and process.

I was given an elegant lunch, with sufficient pre-meal drinks to make the atmosphere congenial. Then I had my interview for the campus radio and with Jim Porter for the University newspaper.

Audiences are very stimulating to me but by the time Jim drove me back to the motel, I was absolutely whacked. He wanted to continue chatting but I told him that I'd run out of energy. I think he was genuinely sorry. He was profuse with invitations to return again, and promised to send me transcripts of the articles and a tape of the radio broadcast.

I didn't think about Dan-the-Mystery-Man until the next morning when I was packing and opened my knitting bag.

Berkeley was next on the itinerary and I was already regretting that I'd agreed to stay with Raymond's sister, Beth. I couldn't retract gracefully because I'd always liked Beth and Foster Hamilton, and their boys. But I suspected I was in for a good deal of reminiscing about Ray, moans about his early, tragic death now a good fourteen years in my past. I didn't mind talking about Ray: I liked to remember him but Beth had a tendency to dwell on the macabre instead of the merry and that is tiring. I needed my energy for the lecturing.

As luck would have it, I arrived in the midst of a family crisis: the older boy, Sam, had been living with a classmate, a girl, and she was pregnant. Should she or should she not get an abortion? I was drafted as an arbitrator which could have been a prickly situation except that I quickly discovered no one really wanted my opinion because I couldn't understand the entire situation, now could I? To which I readily agreed. The crux of the matter was that the girl,

Linda, was afraid that she might be aborting a second Messiah, a genius and 'you could never be sure, could you?' And it really couldn't matter if she'd been smoking hash because they hadn't *proved* it harmed the unborn, now had they?

Foss was out of his depth: Beth was trying to be 'modern' and 'understanding.' I tried to suggest to her that they would solve it themselves among their peers but she couldn't make up her own mind whether she wanted to be a grandmother at thirty-nine or not; or if Linda was wrong about using hash and the child would be a moron. I decided that if Tim ever got into a similar situation—and it was possible—I would insist that the girl carry the child to term. I'd look after it, though it would wreck my writing schedule. I was missing the involvement with someone who depended on *me*. I liked to be needed. I liked to plan around the requirements of someone other than myself. A man would have suited me better but a child would be welcome. Having solved that knotty problem in my own mind, I tried to avoid discussions about Sam and Linda. What *I* would do was not necessarily what *they* would elect.

I was committed to a series of lectures at local community colleges for grade school teachers and library science majors. I could repeat that lecture in my sleep, and almost answer all the questions likely to be generated. In the informal sessions that would crop up after the official lecture, I wondered why I was living on what my writing could bring in when

131

PhD's in my field were pulling in thousands of dollars. I would pull myself up short: I had had that 'glory' before and never more relieved to have the excuse of Tim to pull stakes and replant in Ireland, peaceful, green, haphazard, friendly Ireland.

Easter vacation intervened to let me catch my breath before the second round of junior college talks. I did some sightseeing in San Francisco with Foss, who was delighted to have an excuse to get out of the house. Foss is an associate history professor and a keen war-historian. I'd brought him several Irish textbooks so that he could see how 'our' wars were treated in other history books. We discussed the historical significance of the troubles in Belfast and decided that it would take a massive re-education program to improve the situation which had been in existence for four hundred years.

No sooner were we back in their house than the current war raged about us. Linda was in floods of tears, Beth trying to console her and Sam was glaring at both of them, thoroughly rebellious.

"She's made the appointment—" said Beth defiantly, helplessly.

"Appointment?" Foss was having trouble dragging himself out of the Belfast troubles and its historical significances.

"For the abortion!" Beth's eyes were as wet as Linda's.

"Oh, that!"

I shuddered at Foss' ill-timed diffidence.

"That? Can't you get out of your stuffy history books and into the present needs of your family? These poor children are suffering—"

Foss looked as if he thought he'd done enough suffering and was going to explode. So I did.

"If they're suffering, they brought it on themselves. Furthermore they don't really want to abort the child: it's *theirs!* If they honestly hadn't wanted it, Linda would have gone quietly to the clinic and had it done and over with in twenty-four hours instead of greeting and grembling around here for a week. Have the child! Grow up with it!"

"But . . . but . . . they're in college . . ." Beth began.

"What's that to the point? I was still in school when I had Tim . . ." I saw Beth opening her mouth for another specious argument and jumped on her, aware out of the corner of my eye that Linda had stopped weeping and Sam looked considerably happier. "And don't you dare say things are different. They aren't. And if they have to dump the baby on you while they go to classes, so what? What else are you doing with your time? Think how much fun it'll be to spoil a grandchild. You won't be near as nervous with this one as you were with Sam, or Perry. And he can baby-sit for his nephew. And if it's a girl . . . if you told me once you wanted a girl you told me nineteen times only you couldn't afford a third baby on Foss' salary; if it's a girl, you'd be very pleased. Well, there's nothing wrong with Foss' salary now, al-

though I don't suggest that you two support their baby
. . . but it's obvious to me, though I don't know the
situation as you keep telling me, that no one in this
room wants Linda to abort the child. Now if you'll
excuse me, I have two lectures tomorrow in the boon-
docks and I have to make an early start!''

I made an exit in complete silence but when I had
reached my room, renewal of the conversation in the
living room had a completely different tone. I was
exhausted with that outburst, and trembling. Furthermore, I wondered what on earth had possessed me to
interfere.

I took out my knitting, to calm my nerves, but it
only reminded me of Dan. Well, at least *I* hadn't gotten
pregnant. Then I started to giggle. It was improbable,
but not entirely impossible and wouldn't I look funny
producing at my late age? Would *I* have the courage
to go through with it? It would be Tim's turn to be
sympathetic and understanding . . . having an illegiti-
mate half-brother or sister. I tried to imagine his face
and would he come up with Bawdy Bedside Ballads
for Baby Bastards. My editor would go berserk. I
laughed till the tears came to my eyes and I couldn't
see to knit. I was caught completely unawares by the
knock on the door.

''Yes?''

A radiant Linda and a jubilant Sam stood in my
door. ''We want to thank you, Aunt Dana,'' Linda
said in a tremulous voice. ''We do want the baby.
And furthermore,'' she glanced shyly at Sam, who

seemed to have grown a few inches in the last hour, "we're even going to get married. For real!"

How I kept a straight face for that supreme modern sacrifice I don't know. I had to swallow before I could get any reply past my grin-fixed teeth. I must have come out with an acceptable response for Linda kissed me, Sam shook my hand in a very manly fashion. I must say it was an improvement on the limp grasp he'd given me when I'd arrived.

I had no more recovered my composure from their visitation when Beth arrived, weeping with joy.

"I didn't dare say what you said, Dana. I wanted to, goodness knows, because I simply couldn't stand the idea of Linda . . . aborting . . ." The very notion was repulsive to Beth. ". . . my first grandchild."

"Even Spock was strong on the fact that kids need limits, Beth," I said. "I was only suggesting one . . ."

"But they *listened* to you . . ."

I forebore to mention that I'd said about the same thing . . . more politely . . . when I first arrived.

"Oh, Dana, what would I have done if you hadn't come . . ."

As I didn't know, I said that she would eventually have put her foot down, too. I was sure of it.

"You will stay for the wedding, won't you?" When I started to evade that, she said in a rush, "if you can fit it in with your schedule . . ."

That made it seem ungracious for me to refuse and then she said they'd fit it in with my lecture schedule. I had four more days in the Bay area, didn't I?

I did. And I went to the wedding though to this day I can't remember anything more than Beth, Linda and Linda's mother in floods of tears, mostly happy, I think. I know that the only reason I made the plane to Los Angeles on time was because Foss and Perry deposited me at the proper gate. It wasn't champagne; it was fatigue because I will never again do two lectures a day at community colleges set fifty and two hundred miles apart in sunny California.

When I was unpacking in LA, I found the swimsuit. And thought, again, of Dan. And of the swimming pool reputed to be in the hotel. I made an appointment for my hair, managed ten laps in the pool and then bathed under a sunlamp until it was time to get my hair done. I nearly fell asleep under the hair dryer but contrived to stay awake long enough to get back to my room, into my bed where I conked out and stayed that way until nearly the next morning. My hair-do was no longer perfect but I was a lot better.

Over breakfast the next morning, I brought my 'brains' up to date, and thankfully reviewed a schedule which listed only three more cities after LA. Four more lectures and I could wing my way back to New York, see Tim at college and return, rejoicing, to the unhurried pace of my dear green Ireland.

I wrote to Tim a longish letter before inspiration and energy deserted me. The p.r. man in charge of me in LA rang, and checked the afternoon engagement. As he didn't mention lunch, I ordered a heavenly fruit salad in the hotel.

It's fun being a visiting celebrity up to a point and I reached that point in Los Angeles. By the time I enplaned for Dallas I would have devoutly joined a snow-seeding expedition for another three days of enforced inactivity . . . and no people. The Dallasians (?) showered me with such lavish Texas hospitality . . . at least the beef was barbecued and for real . . . that I crept into Tulsa utterly, completely and thoroughly drained.

I do not remember speaking to the 78 librarians of Whosit County. I do not recall being interviewed on campus TV, though I later received the photos and I *looked* wide awake. I don't remember much of anything in Tulsa except that I must have done it well in my comatose state to judge by the letter of thanks I later received.

I surfaced to the insistent buzzing of the phone, a strident summons that must have been going on for some time to rouse me.

"Mom? Mom, what have you been getting into out West?"

"Tim? Tim?"

"Yeah, Tim, your ever-loving son. Christ, what have you been doing?"

"Sleeping."

"I don't mean now. I thought you knew better."

"Knew what better?"

Tim sounded indignant, angry, upset and very much like his father, trying to be reasonable in a frustrating situation.

"How to keep out of trouble."

"What trouble am I in? And where are you calling?" I had that sudden horrible chill of apprehension. And I couldn't remember where I was.

"I'm calling from Lehigh."

"No, honey, I know where *you* are. What city are you calling me in?"

"Huh? Hey, Mom," and Tim's voice turned anxious. Reflex snapped me out of my daze.

"I'm sorry, honey. I'm sleepy."

"You're in Tulsa, Mom, and you're in trouble."

"What kind? Did I miss a lecture date?"

"No, not that." Tim was disgusted at my obtuseness. "I mean that guy. Lowell."

"Lowell?"

"Yeah, Lowell." Tim was getting angry again, partly relief and partly an inability to get me to function intelligently. "Daniel Jerome Lowell. He's charged with murder and you're his alibi. *He* says. Did you ever meet a Jerry Lowell?"

"Lowell . . . Lowell . . ." I couldn't for the life of me then remember any Lowell but I also didn't remember any murders, or murderers.

"Mother, his lawyer has been trying to catch up with you. So *he* says. I gave him the name of your lecture bureau so they could give him your itinerary. I figured if you *were* involved, you'd better know and if you weren't, you could sue for libel, or something. Only the lawyer has been phoning me saying he keeps

138

leaving messages only you don't answer them. Are you trying to evade him?''

I was still fumbling for the name Lowell.

"What's the lawyer's name?'' That might give me a clue.

"Jefferson, Marshall & Taggert is the firm. Peter Taggert the particular man. Mom, are you sure you're all right?''

"I'm tired, very tired, Timmy. I'm so tired I don't even remember if I've given my talks in Tulsa or I have them to do. What's today's date, please?''

"It's the 10th of April, Mom, and you were to speak in Tulsa on the 8th and 9th. Mom, are you sure you're all right?'' Tim's voice now had the 'small boy in search of security' tone.

"Yes, Tim. I'm just talked out, travelled out and desynch-ed. You woke me out of a sound sleep. You know how I am just waking up.''

"Yeah . . .'' He sounded somewhat reassured.

"So, this Peter Taggert believes I can help his client, a Daniel . . . Dan!''

"You do know him?'' My admission startled Tim more than my bleary state of mind.

"Denver Dan-the-man. Yes, I know Dan, and he isn't a murderer. I don't see how he could have murdered anyone . . . I mean. When? Who? Why?''

"I don't know many details, Mother, except that it happened in Denver . . . Is he that swimming-hiking freak you wrote me about?'' Tim wasn't certain that

139

these were sufficient *bona fides*. "Haven't you seen the papers?"

"Papers! I've been on tour. I'm lucky to get to read menus."

"He's supposed . . . alleged is the word they use . . . alleged to have killed his former wife on Thursday, March 20. She wasn't found for two days because of the snow but he's supposed to have killed her approximately 11 PM Thursday evening."

As Tim talked, I had been thumbing through my diary. Thursday was the last evening we had spent together . . . and at 11 PM we'd been watching Gunga Din . . . No, we hadn't. We'd been making love. But that was irrelevant to the fact that Dan Lowell had been most decidedly in my company the entire evening.

"He was with me all Thursday evening, Tim. What do I do now?"

"I suggest that you call the legal man. He *said* he'd been trying to reach you. He's phoned me three times because you're the only proof his client didn't murder the woman. Plenty of circumstantial evidence to prove that he could have."

"He couldn't have and he wouldn't have. He's not that kind of guy."

"Call the man." There was relief in Tim's voice for my positive statement. "When will I see you?"

"I'd planned to fly back tomorrow but now . . ."

"You'd better let justice triumph, Mom. I'll see ya when I see ya!"

It was ten-thirty Rocky Mountain time. As I dialed

140

the number Tim had given me, I recalled receiving
message slips at the last two hotels. They hadn't
made any sense to me at the time. I had stuffed them
in my case and sure enough, they were all from a
Peter Taggert, and they informed me, classically, that
it was a matter of life and death.

"My name is . . . Jenny Lovell," I told Taggert's
receptionist in Denver. "I believe Peter Taggert wants
to get in touch with me."

"Miss Lovell? Just a mo . . . *Mrs. Lovell?*" The
girl reacted violently. "He is, but he isn't here. Oh,
he's in court with Mr. Lowell. Oh, where are you,
please? Babs," this was said to someone at her end,
"she's calling in. It's her. Hold on, Mrs. Lovell, for
Mr. Taggert's secretary."

"Mrs. Lovell? Where are you calling from, please?"
The second girl was more in command of herself but I
could hear the undercurrent of excitement and relief
in her tone.

"Right now I'm in Tulsa but I can be in Denver as
soon as I can get a plane. Will that help?"

"Yes, it will. Your presence here is urgently
needed."

"Look, I'm terribly, terribly sorry I didn't call
earlier. My son just rang me. I haven't read any
newspapers in days. You're sort of in a limbo when
you're touring. If I'd known . . . I mean, Dan Lowell
wouldn't kill anyone. I've never heard of anything so
outrageous. My son said that he's supposed to have
killed his former wife at 11 on Thursday evening and

141

you tell Mr. Taggert *I* know he didn't. He was with me the entire evening. Things haven't gone too far, have they?''

''Just come to Denver, Mrs. Lovell. Your testimony is vitally needed.''

''I'll be on the next plane. And look, would you tell Mr. Lowell that . . . Gunga Din is bringing the water?''

''I beg your pardon?''

I repeated my remark which then didn't sound too witty but Dan would appreciate the reference and I couldn't think of anything else that didn't sound trite and insincere.

''There must be a plane out of here for Denver sometime today, and I'll be on it. Be sure of that. Okay?''

She asked for and I gave her the present Tulsa number but as soon as I disconnected that call, I got the flight reservations desk. I had missed a morning flight from Tulsa but I could book on the 2 PM. I packed in a flap, remembering to cash one of the lecture checks where I was known. At that, I had to get a bit huffy with the manager because he wouldn't believe that I didn't have any credit cards apart from my Allied Irish Bank cheque-cashing ident. I had to ask him, in my most acid tones, didn't he think the University's checks were any good so he demurred and grudgingly handed over the money. I noticed he used dirty bills and small ones so I had an unwieldy wad. Then I overtipped the bellboy and doorman as I got in the cab for the airport.

There was no trouble in altering my ticket to include a stopover in Denver but I had two hours to wait until I could board the plane: plenty of time to stew. I found a Denver paper on the newsstand but there was no follow-up yarn about the murder: no mention of it at all.

Had Tim had the facts straight? Thursday? I riffled through the diary. Most of Dan's time those three days had been spent in my company, except for a few brief hours, especially that Thursday evening. He'd been with Hearty-har-har when he hadn't been with me. Had Tim said 11 PM? Dan was covered as far as the AM was concerned, too, because . . . yes . . . we were swimming at 10 AM Thursday. Of course, he could have nipped out after I'd gone to sleep Thursday evening late, or was it by then Friday morning . . . but how far away had his ex-wife lived?

Dan had been worried about something. Worried? Anxious? Annoyed? Betrayed? Yes, that had been the elusive quality about his mood that evening: he'd been angry and felt betrayed. By his former wife?

I shook my head. This line of thought was unproductive. And disturbing. I had too few facts beyond the major one: Dan had been in my company most of those snow-bound days, his time accounted for when he wasn't. Besides which, he wasn't a murderer.

I recognized that anyone can be pushed to the point

143

of murder. But Dan acted like a driven or trapped man, unless he was far more a dissembler than I could give him credit for. And, he'd had *two* tickets in the airport that afternoon. Furthermore, at lunch he had definitely acted relieved, as if he'd solved his problem. Solved his problem by escaping the scene of the crime? No, no. He'd been with me at the reported time of the murder!

I killed (whooops . . .) passed some time eating a good lunch in the airport restaurant, complete with a half bottle of wine for its soothing quality. Anger is a good therapy and I was angry on many counts: angry at Tim's being involved at all in this; angry at myself for not having appreciated the genuine urgency in the messages from Taggert; angry at the unknown murderer who had involved Dan, me, and Tim in such a ghastly affair. Angry because my very lovely brief encounter was now besmirched.

I resolutely took out my knitting as I settled myself to wait to board the plane. That reminded me of how I had got into Dan's company in the first place. But the knitting worked its usual charm. I reviewed and re-reviewed what I did know about Dan, and Denver, and my conclusion reaffirmed my judgment of him. He was innocent of that capital charge.

I was overwhelmingly grateful to be asked to board at Gate 9. I was glad to be involved with the routine of flying, responding to the hostess's polite queries. And wondering what would happen if I told her, instead of inanities, that I was flying to Denver as the material witness in a murder case. Trial? No, it hadn't, it couldn't have come to trial so soon. Could it? But my flight was really a matter of someone's life which was being threatened by someone else's death.

VIII

WHEN I WALKED UP THE RAMP in Denver, I had graduated from Visiting Celebrity to Murder Witness. This makes for flash photos and newspaper reporters and an entirely different sort of reception I'd rather not endure again.

Fortunately Peter Taggert was there. After my first confusion of shouting 'no comment' my arm was grabbed by a stocky man in an elegant pinstripe suit with one of those expensive patterned tie and shirt combinations. He elbowed two reporters out of the

149

way and placed his broad back between me and the other important members of the press.

"I'm Pete Taggert, Mrs. Lovell, if you'll come with me." He ran interference. "No comment, boys. You can see Mrs. Lovell later. Right now, I got her. This way, Mrs. Lovell." He seemed to plow/bam/crash on my name. But he could pow/bam/crash through the reporters.

"Give me your baggage checks, Mrs. Lovell," he said to me in an undertone as we raced down the slick corridor.

He gave them in turn to someone running beside us and then veered suddenly to our right, through a door marked 'private,' down some steps leading to a corridor, through a door to the back VIP parking. He guided me to a big, dark green Buick convertible. We were away, zooming out of the airport, neat as you please.

There were still snowdrifts lining the roads.

"First, Mrs. Lovell, thanks for calling today. You're saving Jerry's life. Second, let me apologize for dragging your son into this but that was the only clue we had to your whereabouts without a police search. I don't think guest lecturers would appreciate that kind of attention. Jerry'd seen your son's address on a letter. He wanted me to get that straight with you first. Third, having got you here I'd better tell you that this is going to be a nasty case."

He kept his eyes on the road as he talked so that I had only his rather rough profile to look at and no indication of his attitude or feelings. He drove fast but well and spoke in a low, well placed voice which was conversational rather than obviously controlled.

"There've been some snide cracks about your existence, Mrs. Lovell . . ."

"Why did you emphasize my name so heavily at the airport?"

"Jerry said you were quick . . ." He grinned.

"I also know him as Dan rather than Jerry . . ."

"So he said. About your name, *his* is Lowell."

"Close but no cigar . . ."

"Not when you see the handwriting on your room bill. It *looks* like Lowell. Clerk error, okay, but the prosecution is making out that you knew each other before; that your presence in the hotel was pre-arranged . . ."

"*And* the murder?"

"The alibi was pre-arranged . . . so the murder could be committed with impunity."

I felt cold and a bit sick.

"I suppose we arranged the snowstorm, too?"

"They'd like it if you had." Peter Taggert's mouth curved down in a sour smile.

"I'd never met Dan . . . Jerry . . . Lowell before in my life. After all, I can prove I'd been living in Ireland . . ."

He shot me a surprised look. "You don't know what he does for a living?"

"He said someting about being an engineer and travelling a lot."

151

"And you don't read Irish newspapers? About off-shore oil?"

"Oh, God, and he has been in Ireland?"

He nodded slowly, his eyes on the road.

"So Dan and I were supposed to have met in Dublin, hatched up a murder, seeded clouds for a convenient blizzard for what reason? If they were already divorced?"

"Noreen Sue . . ."

"Good God, I didn't think people were really named that."

"Noreen Sue divorced Jerry two years ago, and bluntly, took him for all she could. Part of the settlement was her right to use the marital home . . . which has been in Dan's family since Pike discovered the Peak—as long as she remained in Denver with their son. Jerry wanted DJ to have a settled life." Peter Taggert snorted. "Noreen's nothing but a tramp and the boy's been miserable. He's only just old enough to appeal to court to change the custody. The case is . . . was due . . . to come up in two weeks . . ."

"Then you were one of his business phone calls?"

"Yes . . ." he was about to say more but changed his mind.

"And she was fighting the matter?"

"Yes, with all she had. She'd lose the house and the support money. I don't think she cared about losing the boy . . ."

"I'd say that *she* had reason to murder him . . . not

152

the other way around. You haven't told me how she was killed?''

"She was hit on the head and died of exposure."

"That's not murder . . .''

"No, manslaughter. But if they can prove Jerry did it, it'll put him into jail for a long time and deprive him of his son.''

"The poor boy! And where was he at the time?'' I am not fond of calling kids by initials; it sounds affected.

"DJ was in Denver with a school friend. His mother was supposed to pick him up Tuesday after school when the blizzard warnings were hoisted but she never collected him.''

"Where was the marital home . . . in relation to the airport hotel?''

"On the way into Denver, Mrs. Lovell. About three miles from the hotel . . . as the snow bird flies.''

I began to see the problem. "In short, Dan—had he been the killer—could have hiked from the hotel to the house, done the dirty and come back in spite of the weather conditions?''

"Yes.''

"Too bad that won't wash. Dan was never out of my sight, particularly on the night involved, long enough to have hiked three miles in those conditions.''

"Prosecution has a witness who saw him at the hotel at 6 PM dressed for outdoors, found him very distracted and anxious to get away.''

153

Anne McCaffrey

"Old Hearty-har-har . . ."

"I beg your pardon?"

"That's what I called . . . oh, what was his name
. . . I have it written down in my diary."

"Fred B. Winkleman?"

"Fred, yes, that was what Dan called him. I was at
the elevator when Dan was trying to shake him loose."

"You were?"

"Yes, I was. And I was in Dan's company . . ." I
took a deep breath, ". . . the entire night. We watched
both screenings of Gunga Din: that was the feature
film of the week."

"Gunga Din?" His foot slipped on the accelerator.

"Yes, and I'd swear to that under oath, on a stack
of Bibles, anything you wish."

"Yes, Mrs. Lovell."

My willingness did not seem to reassure him. He
sounded tired, morally tired.

"So it's on Hearty-har-har's say-so that Dan is
pegged for the role of murderer? That seems rather
flimsy evidence."

"I said it was all circumstantial. There's a night
watchman that spoke with him at 4:30 AM Friday,
who said he was fully dressed."

"Yes, but . . ."

"There are statements that Noreen Sue was aware
that Dan was in Denver, at that hotel, and she had
telephoned several people, asking them to come stay
with her because she was afraid of what Dan might do
to her."

154

"Hysterical type. And?"

"The storm prevented anyone from getting to her house."

"Oh?"

"She also phoned the police, saying that she was in physical danger from her ex-husband. He had called her . . . the calls are part of the hotel records . . ."

"Yes, they would be . . ."

"Dan says he phoned to speak to DJ, and she wouldn't let him."

"You said DJ wasn't even in the house."

"That's right but Dan said Noreen Sue didn't tell him that."

"Mr. Taggert, he had two tickets in his hand when we got to the airport on Friday . . ."

The lawyer's lips set briefly in a thin, angry line. "Jerry was taking DJ to San Francisco with him. He'd found out . . . from me . . . that DJ had been with the McPhersons during the blizzard. He felt, and I concurred with him, that Noreen Sue was not a fit guardian for the boy and he would resume custody of him until the hearing."

"And?" Because it was apparent somehow this was wrong.

"This has been construed to mean that Jerry knew that Noreen Sue was no longer alive to take care of the boy."

"Oh!" Yes, I could see how that could be assumed. "Well, then, who did bang Noreen Sue on the bean

155

and leave her to die? Because it bloody hell wasn't Dan!''

He gave me a warm smile for my outburst.

"Don't you believe me? Him?''

"I do, yes.''

"Well, aren't there other suspects? Surely there were vandals and thieves out in the blizzard, getting what they could? Or an irate boyfriend of hers? Or maybe she was just . . . blown down, and hit her head? Slipped on the ice?''

"Unfortunately the prosecution rather fancies their case against Jerry.''

"Well, I'm here now. They have no case against him. I was with Dan all night!''

He sighed. "That's just it, Mrs. Lovell, without meaning any offense.''

"What is it?''

He sighed, swinging about a rotary. "Did you have sexual relations with my client, Mrs. Lovell?''

"Yes, I did.''

He gave me another fast inscrutable look.

"Although to be utterly candid, that should support his alibi rather than deny it.''

"It should.'' He sounded horribly unsure.

"At my age, Mr. Taggert, I've got too much sense to be sentimental about sex. Or to perjure myself.''

He didn't answer immediately as he was steering the big car into a parking lot by an older office building. We were, I presumed, in the business section of Denver.

"That's just it, Mrs. Lovell," he said, putting on the handbrake. "The prosecution is likely to suggest that at your age, you might do anything for sex. Jerry's a good-looking guy . . ."

I remember having to close my mouth because the cold crisp air of Denver got in as he opened his door. By the time he had opened mine, I was really burning mad. I stalked beside him into the building, seething with fury, impervious to the cold, and tapping my foot on the carpeted elevator as we were silently wafted up to whatever floor his offices were on.

"How do you know that's what they'd try to prove, Mr. Taggert?" I said when we were in his corridor and alone.

He indicated an anonymous door in the corridor that ended in an imposing glass partition with the firm's name in discreet gold leaf. Beyond I noticed a reception area, western in treatment and modern in execution.

He ushered me into his private office, leather stuffed seats, huge heavy leather bound law tomes, a desk with neat piles of paper and a yellow-lined note-pad, full of pencilled phrases, askew on the blotter.

"I know the prosecution, Mrs. Lovell. They're out to get Jerry if they can because they have a possible motive and can prove opportunity. They will try to establish that you are perjuring yourself."

"But I'm not. . . . Certainly not on the basis of a couple of good tumbles in bed!"

"The hotel staff mentioned a woman in his company on and off. Noreen Sue was, at the time of her death, a blonde, about your size and height, Mrs. Lovell . . .''

"Good God, doesn't the truth count for anything anymore?"

"Sometimes I wonder, Mrs. Lovell. I really do. Right now, I'd like to take down your version . . . all right, the truth . . . of the critical time. Stick to the facts only, please." He depressed a toggle on his intercom and asked his secretary to come in.

"The facts, huh? The version according to Mrs. Lovell? The truth as I see it?"

He gave me a tight smile for my sour parody on the sensational press type headlines. I was repentant for his eyes were tired and cynical. I sensed he was desperately afraid for Jerry-Dan yet here was I, his hope for Dan's reprieve, likely to jeopardize the matter still more. His secretary came in, pad in hand, and sat with quiet attention after giving me a composed nod and smile of greeting.

"I'll need my diary," I said, unlatching my attaché case. "My brains," I rattled on, trying to lighten the atmosphere. I opened it to the proper pages and looked first at his secretary and then him in expectation. "I'm ready."

"Details first, like your name . . .''

"My full name is Dana Jane Lovell. I'm sorry, Dana Jane Hartman Lovell. I use D.J. Hartman for my professional papers . . .''

"Professional papers?" He held up his hand to his secretary to suspend dictation.

"Yes, I have my PhD in Library Sciences and I often publish in Library Journals, and some teachers' magazines, library skills, that sort of thing . . ." I paused because Peter Taggert was staring at me. "What's the matter?"

"You really have a PhD?"

"I don't carry the diploma around but you can check with Columbia University in New York. Or in the *Who's Who of American Women*. I've been listed since 1970." And that was the first time I'd ever called on that for a reference.

"You're a real, *bona fide* doctor of philosophy?" He was still incredulous.

"Yes, I am. But it is in library sciences, not . . ."

He waved an impatient hand at my attempt to qualify. "You've a masters in what?"

"Education."

"Did you teach?"

"Yes, but I didn't really like it . . ."

"Where?" He wanted the facts, just the facts but he was excited . . . and more, hopeful.

"In Cambridge while my husband was getting his doctorate in Sociology at Harvard. And then I taught after Raymond died."

"Raymond was your husband? How did he die?"

"He died of cancer of the lungs fourteen years ago."

"You've only the one child?"

159

"Yes, Tim's nineteen now."

"You never remarried?" He had held up his hand briefly to signal his secretary to hold the dictation.

"No," and then I grinned at the half-formed question in his expression. "I've had offers and I've had lovers. But writing's a full-time occupation, Mr. Taggert, and I've a son to get through college, and that takes too much time."

"Writer? I thought you were a teacher. Oh, yes, you said you write for journals. . . . Now, let's just get the statement. Barbara?" He glanced at his secretary. "Go ahead, Dr. Lovell." And he grinned at me as he emphasized the title.

Again I reduced the facts of a tender love-affair to a dry recitation of times and activities. It sounded worse when Barbara read back the dictation, and absolutely sexless. Which was to Mr. Taggert's satisfaction for he sat there nodding and steepling his fingers. When Barbara had finished speaking, he smiled, leaning back in his chair and idly swinging it on its gimbals.

"Good, good. Would you type that please, Barbara?"

She murmured, nodded pleasantly to me, the modern efficient paragon of a legal secretary and left the room.

"Things are looking much better, Doctor Lovell. Yes, indeed!"

"A difference in degree?"

He bellowed so appreciatively that his secretary poked her head back through the door to inquire if he'd called. He waved her an okay.

160

"Yes, it does, Doctor Lovell."

"You mean, PhD's can have affairs with impunity. It's just not done by fuzzy-minded housewives on a mid-winter holiday and hot enough in the knickers to lay anything?"

He shook both head and hands, laughing.

"And PhD's only indulge in erudite discourse and sexless physical exercise?"

"Something like that, Doctor Lovell. Something more like that! Did Jerry know?"

"About my doctorate? The subject of academic degrees never arose."

"Hmmm. Yes. Of course. Might I have a look at your diaries? I see you have last year's with you as well."

"I had a lecture tour then too and I brought it along for my notes."

"I see." He started with the current diary and I watched, a bit self-conscious but amused at the various expressions crossing his face as he turned the pages. I kept wondering what I had written that would delight him under the circumstances.

"What does D or C mean?"

I hid my mouth in my hand. "That's rather personal, Mr. Taggert."

His expression invited me to confide.

"I have trouble switching water supplies . . . the D means diarrhea, the C . . ."

"I get it."

"Trivia, Mr. Taggert."

"Hmmm, but in its own elementary . . ."

"Mr. Taggert!"

"Sorry about that. I do love to pun. In its way, however, Doctor Lovell, such trivia *supports* the relevant entries." He flicked through the pages, noting that I kept more or less the same sort of annotations and abbreviations, nodding his head more and more vigorously.

"I underlined the names and references I'd need this year in green ink."

"I had wondered about that." He gave a deep, satisfied sigh. "I'm not a dairist myself but I thank God you are. These entries are obviously made almost daily. Tim is your son?" I nodded. "And who is Mairead?"

"My closest friend in Dublin."

"And SK?"

"My agent."

"PS?"

"One of my publishers."

"Desmond?"

"A personal friend."

"Ah, then you always designate business or professional people by their initials and your personal friends by their first or full name?"

"Generally."

"And I do not see a prior reference to either a DJL or a Jerry or a Dan in either. On this sort of trivia," and he waggled the diaries at me, "cases are made or broken. Mathews' contention that you knew Jerry

162

prior to Denver is blown!'' He swung back and forth in the gimballed chair, very pleased.

"I have to be a bit personal, Doctor Lovell. What did you and Jerry talk about? Did he mention how worried he was about his son? Or why he was in Denver?''

"No, although I knew something was worrying him. Actually, we didn't talk much . . . yes, I know, Mr. Taggert, we were otherwise occupied but only some of the time . . . I'd just had three weeks of lectures and discussions and I really wanted not to have to answer questions or talk about myself or my work or anything. Dan was of a like mind but I see now that his real worries were to come. We simply did not get involved in each other's personal lives. He did say he was divorced and he did mention a son. So did I but the comments were in passing. We did discuss the weather, our fellow passengers, swimming, hiking, how to cheat at card games, inconsequentialities. But no details given, or asked.''

"Unfortunately the dearth of detail about you went against him. He only knew that you were a lecturer, lived in Ireland, widowed and . . .'' he paused, dropping his eyes to the floor where my knitting bag rested, "never dropped stitches when you knit.''

"Have you spoken to Dan since my phone call?''

Mr. Taggert had a very engaging smile when he wasn't worried or cynical. "He got the message about the water, Doctor Lovell, and you couldn't have said anything to revive him faster. He's been pretty depressed and hopeless, I can tell you.''

"He didn't think I'd deliberately let him down?''

Peter Taggert eyed me for a long moment. "No. He didn't. He insisted that you probably hadn't got the message or understood it. I was to refer to him as Dan, not Jerry.''

"Why is he Jerry and not Dan, if his name is Daniel Jerome?''

"The Second. His father was known as Dan Lowell.''

"So the son is number three?''

There was a discreet knock at the door and his secretary re-entered, typed sheets floating in her hand.

"I've called the notary public, Mr. Taggert, and he'll wait for you.''

"Good.'' Mr. Taggert only seemed to glance at the pages and he grinned openly at the last one, slipping it over to me first. I was clearly identified as Dana Jane Hartman Lovell, BA, MA, PhD.

"Read it through and see if you have anything to add. Or delete.''

I read slowly, every word. I meant, and reaffirmed every word of my testimony. And said so. He slipped it into a manila folder.

"Thanks for staying over, Babs.''

"I was more than glad to, Mr. Taggert. Anything for Mr. Lowell and DJ.'' She smiled broadly at me, not a bit efficient-secretary, and then left the room.

The lawyer helped me on with my cloak and sug-

gested I bring my things with me but could he keep
the diaries for the moment. I agreed.

The notary public was a scrawny little man who
kept a sporting goods shop two blocks away from the
office. He rattled through the statement under his
breath, ohed a bit at my titles, and then had me swear
that I'd told the truth. I signed the documents in his
presence, he stamped it all right and tight and handed
the thing back to Peter Taggert, taking his fee in the
other hand and palming the bill into his pocket in a
fluid gesture. From practice, I guess.

"I've booked you into a central city hotel, Dr.
Lovell."

"How long will the wheels of justice take now?"

"That depends on what Jack Mathews, our keen
sighted, charge sticking D.A. thinks of this affidavit.
Which he will have on his desk in the morning. Good
God, you don't have more lectures to give, have
you?"

"No, Tulsa was the end of this year's round."

"That's all to the good."

Something in his tone brought me up sharp. "Why?"

"Oh, something could be construed that you're
doing this for publicity purposes."

I stared at him, snapping my mouth shut when I
realized that my jaw had dropped. "For college
lectures? Whose side are you on?"

"Jerry's. And yours. But I know the D.A. His
situation with more crimes and fewer arrests, a pressure from the governor to keep Denver decent, makes

him snatch on anything he can pin to a criminal.
He's got a b'ar hunt in Jerry. And the two have never
liked each other . . .''

"Personal vendetta? What is it the Mafia have, a
contract?"

We had drawn up in front of a glass and brick hotel
entrance. Peter Taggert leaned forward to peer past
me through the entrance. With a muttered oath, he
pressed down on the accelerator and we took off. I'd
been in the process of opening my door; now I clung
to the handle, hoping it wouldn't swing wide.

"Hey, my door."

"Close it! Please." He added the courtesy after the
snapped order.

"What's wrong?"

"Reporters. I'd rather they didn't have a go at
you."

"Why? Wouldn't Doctor Lovell be sufficient?"

"I don't think you need the shit."

"I think you're quite right," I replied after a
moment's reflection. I'd learned quite enough today
to unsettle me and I was angry enough, seething
inside, to be indiscreet out of simple complicated
frustration.

I didn't ask him where he was taking me now. I
was too depleted, deflated and depressed. Running to
someone's rescue is stimulating; you're full of do-
goodery, uprightness, moral rectitude and honest anger.
When you've done your bit, the reaction is equally
severe and devastating. I resolved never to tour again,

or knit on board a plane, or converse with total strangers, male or female, however charming and whatever the circumstances.

"Having second thoughts, Doctor?"

"Thoughts, yes. But nothing to deflect me from my present course, Mr. Taggert. I don't renege on my given word. Or my sworn statement."

"You were telling the truth?"

"The whole truth and nothing but the truth, unpalatable and somewhat unflattering."

"Unflattering?"

"Sure, Gunga Din had more of his attention than I!"

I succeeded in making Peter Taggert chuckle.

"I like you, lady."

"Get Daniel Jerome Lowell cleared of this ridiculous charge and I'll return the compliment."

"Not until then?"

"We'll see, particularly if you will tell me where you're taking me now."

"Where I can protect my star witness."

With superb timing he turned the Buick up a drive, leading to a low, spread out ranch-type house in the couple of hundred thousand dollar bracket. From snow-covered lumps evenly spaced along the drive, I could imagine that in the summer the place was magnificently landscaped. Lights glowed in the main entrance but the other glass windows were draped and impenetrable. We swung past the main entrance to a triple car garage and one of the doors silently moved

167

upwards. The Buick slid in and the door, down. I'd forgotten such amenities and must have looked my surprise.

"The part of American life most likely to be forgotten in Ireland," I said to Peter Taggert as he grinned at my expression.

A side door opened and a tiny elegant woman was silhouetted against the light.

"Peter? Did she really come?"

"She really came and she's also here. The reporters had gathered at the hotel."

"Mrs. Lovell, do come . . . ."

"She's officially Doctor Lovell, Petra. Dana Jane Lovell, my wife, Petra."

As I walked towards the woman, my mind boggled over Peter-Petra but the moment our hands clasped, both of her small ones around mine, I forgot all in her radiant welcome. She was genuinely overjoyed to see me. She kept shaking my hand as she led me into the side hall, repeating how glad she was I'd come, that the messages had reached me, and was I very tired? Would I like a drink? Did I wish to freshen up first?

I kept saying yes, and enthusiastically "yes" for the drink. I needed it more urgently when Petra escorted me into the huge living room and Daniel Jerome Lowell rose from a black leather chair beside the immense western ranch style fireplace.

"Jenny! You came!"

"You did drop a few stitches, my friend . . ."

I hoped that my voice sounded casual but my in-

168

nards were executing some peculiar gyrations. All the rationalizations, stern moral warnings and careful interpretations of three snow-bound days in Denver went up the flue with the smoke of the great fire burning there.

I hadn't expected to see him. I mean, I thought he would be stuck in jail.

"You can arrange bail on manslaughter charges, you know," Peter said quietly in my ear and then led me towards the fire. "You're freezing. Get the woman a drink, Jerry. Be useful. She is."

I managed to respond to the pleasantries, to thank Dan for the drink he brought me, to nod and smile as Peter Taggert, all skepticism and sour cynicism gone, itemized the strengths of my supporting evidence.

Dan was equally surprised at my title and quirked his eyebrows at me deferentially, but that was his only flash of the wayward humor I'd enjoyed. This ghastly business had left ineradicable marks on him, to his eyes, the downward pull of his mouth, the set of his shoulders: not defeated, but as if he was expecting more psychological blows to fall and steeling himself to endure. As Peter discounted each of the points of circumstantial evidence against Dan in the light of my statement, Dan visibly straightened and began to relax. Instead of sitting in a stiff way in the comfortable chair, he slowly leaned back, slid down and finally stretched out his legs and crossed them at the ankles. The merest touch of a smile drew his

169

mouth up as he looked across the hearth at me, raised his glass in a toast. I shrugged a disclaimer.

"Well, I *am* glad," said Petra abruptly, "but I think we're being terribly inconsiderate of Doctor Lovell. She's been travelling and I'm sure she'd like to freshen up before dinner." She rose and gestured gracefully to me. "Please do excuse our inhospitality because you're the answer to our most fervent prayers."

She led me from the lounge which was the center of the L-shaped house, past the main entrance foyer, up steps to what was the bedroom level.

"It's been so ghastly because everything pointed to Jerry and I knew, I just knew, he couldn't have struck Noreen Sue. God knows he's had provocation; that's why he stayed away . . ."

A door whipped open and a boy catapulted into the hall.

"She came?" He did not bear much facial resemblance to his father but something about the haunted intensity of expression evoked Daniel Jerome.

"Yes, DJ, I came. I'm sorry I didn't realize sooner that I was needed. You must have been very worried."

He planted himself squarely in front of me, cocking his head which was a mannerism of his father's, all right enough.

"You were with him? Watching Gunga Din, like he said?"

"You father told the truth, DJ. In fact, we saw the whole film twice."

He gave an exaggerated sigh of relief. Then stuck

his hand out at me, his face wreathed with a happy smile. "I'm Daniel Jerome Lowell the Third."

"I'm . . . Dana Jane Lovell . . . Doctor of Philosophy." We solemnly shook hands.

"A doctor? Of philosophy?" The first condition awed him; he wasn't sure of the second but he gave me a long searching look. "What does that mean?"

"Dr. Lovell can tell you *after* she's freshened up, DJ. It's nearly time for dinner now."

"Dana? Is that female for Daniel?"

I didn't know and said so.

"But, gee, your initials are the same as mine, and my dad's."

"DJ," said Petra warningly.

"I guess I better wash now. Excuse me." He sort of bounced on the balls of his feet back to his room, obviously in much better frame.

I was gladder than ever that I'd come, and truly dismayed that I had ignored the previous messages. That boy had suffered deeply and all through my stupidity.

"The young are resilient," Petra said.

"He's still too young to have to endure sordidness."

She showed me into a white-walled room, small, simple but restful with its Indian motifs, and flicked on the switch in the adjoining bathroom. I had about ten minutes before dinner, she said and left me.

Stimulation had given a false animation to my face. I stared at my tired reflection in the mirror, observing that the only thing alive about my face was my hair

171

which gleamed silver-orange in the vanity light. Vigorously I washed my face and put on fresh make-up. Some improvement. I splashed on some of my Graffiti cologne. That helped, too. Good perfume ranks with a fresh hair-do as a great morale booster.

I could hear the laughter of young girls as I retraced my steps to the living room. When I entered, silence fell as Dan and Peter Taggert got to their feet. DJ nudged the girl nearest him. Her black pigtails bounced as she whipped her head around. The other girl was already facing me; they both stared at me as if I were coming out in green stripes.

"Dr. Lovell, these are my daughters, Pierrot and Alexandra," said Peter.

"*Are* you the Dana Jane Lovell who writes the 'Timmy' books?" Pierrot's words rushed out of her mouth as if I'd better be that Dana Jane Lovell. "There can't be two people with that name!"

"I am!"

"Oh?" My affirmative was greeted with such excited bliss that what could have been an awkward situation was covered by frantic questions from both girls. Was there really a Timmy? Did he really get into those exciting situations? Did he really think up all those creatures? Or dream them? Did I have a picture of Timmy? Could they see it after supper? Was I writing any more 'Timmy' books? What was the next one about?

Petra, coming from the kitchen to announce that dinner was ready, had to shush her daughters long enough to be heard. The girls each grabbed a hand, chattering a mile a minute, to lead me into the dining room so Petra surrendered to happy chance and seated me between the two girls instead of Dan and Peter.

"Dr. Lovell . . ." Peter began, holding up a hand to quiet his daughters.

"I'd prefer to be . . . Jenny, please. I never use the title."

"The title is an essential in Denver, Jenny. Now, I don't mean to sound ignorant"—his daughters giggled— "but are your children's books as popular as my daughters lead me to suspect?"

"They are pretty widely read."

"And librarians would know your name?"

"I believe so."

"Mrs. Harrison knows her name," Pierrot said, stoutly my champion. She was the clinging type and I'd had to disengage myself from her clasp to eat. "Our school library has every single one of the 'Timmy' books and two of some."

I began to see the method behind his question.

"Thank God you're not a Jacqueline Susann," he said, rolling his eyes expressively.

"I wish I could laugh all the way to the bank the way she does . . . did."

"Not in this case."

I saw Petra gesture minutely with one hand, noticed Peter catch her eye and nod.

"And what happened in school today, Pierrot?"

173

Petra asked her daughter, firmly establishing that business was not to be discussed at dinner.

I didn't mean to dominate the dinner conversation but Pierrot and Zandra vied with each other in asking 'Timmy' questions; some of them so outrageous that even Dan laughed. I was conscious of his gaze and DJ's rapt expression. The boy early admitted, somewhat gruffly, that he had never read any of my books but would Pierrot lend him one for after his homework? He was relieved to learn that Timmy was grown-up, and quite respectful when I told them that Tim was studying to be an engineer at Lehigh.

Peter Taggert was passive to the conversation's flow, even after I'd finally got the children off the subject of Tim and onto winter sports. The lawyer was deep in some private reflections, though he joined in laughter and seemed to follow what was being said. Petra kept glancing at me, too, but that was more to see if the children were bothering me with their questions. Dan slouched in his chair, his shoulders sagging. He kept playing with the silverware at his place, starting suddenly and pulling himself erect in a conscious effort to appear part of the group. Son kept one eye on Father all through dinner. DJ III adored DJ II.

After dinner the children were firmly sent to their rooms to do their homework, with Petra physically shooing them to the steps of the bedroom level.

"Now then," she said with an exaggerated sigh of

relief, "we can have coffee in peace. And I need a brandy."

"Let me," Dan said, striding to the bar cabinet.

"I'll bring in the coffee," said Peter and his wife winked at me as she settled, with another sigh, into a chair by the fire, curling her legs under her. She looked tinier than ever in the large chair.

"Has this mess interrupted your lecture tour?" Dan asked, passing around the brandy snifters.

"No, I finished in Tulsa. Or maybe Tulsa finished me. And I do want to explain why I didn't answer Peter's message sooner. I was getting so I didn't know where I was, what city, what college, what time . . ."

Dan pressed my hand, all too briefly, and smiled reassuringly.

"I told Peter that's probably what was happening . . ."

"I'm so glad to see you . . ."

"You mean, outside the pokey?"

"I didn't know. I've never been . . ."

"I wouldn't have dragged you into this if I could have . . ."

"I don't bloody mind, Dan!" I was furious with him for being so goddamn anxious.

"He wouldn't cooperate at first," said Peter grimly, returning with the coffee tray, "just in case you think the age of chivalry is dead, Jenny."

"There wasn't any need at first to involve Jenny . . ."

"Until a neighbor remembered seeing a man in a ski mask around the house . . ." Peter growled in his

175

throat. "And Fred . . . do you know Jenny calls him Hearty-har-har, Petra?"

"Oh, heavens, but that's perfect . . ." murmured Petra as her husband continued.

". . . Fred remembered the ski mask in Jerry's pocket."

"Do I refer to you as Jerry? Or Dan?" I asked.

"I can't change Pete at this late date but I'd prefer you to call me Dan . . ." A darkness closed briefly over his face and I'd the notion that his ex-wife had called him "Jerry" in such a way as to make him wish for the change.

"I'll try, man, I'll try," Peter said in a gravelly voice.

"So what are my chances, Peter, now that we've involved Jenny in the case?"

Peter took a long drag on his cigar (at least he wasn't inhaling) and saw my inadvertent reaction. "Does smoking bother you?"

"Only because of what I've seen it do, and know it can do. I apologize if my thoughts were that transparent."

"Peter *tried* to give it up," Petra said, "but he's under such strain . . ."

"You're not inhaling . . ." I tried to mitigate my unspoken anxiety. "What are Dan's chances now?"

"As I told you in the office, Jenny, and as Dan knows, it depends on how much weight the D.A. will give your statement. There's a good hunk of circumstantial evidence against Jer . . . Dan. Opportunity, unfortunately, is there and Mathews has it that the custody bit provides a motive. Noreen Sue certainly did blab it about that she was terrified of what Daniel J might do. Jerry has admitted, and it's a matter of record, that he telephoned her several times: that his primary reason in stopping off in Denver was to see DJ and find out exactly what truth there was behind the boy's letters that Noreen Sue was having wild parties in the house which kept him up all night, that she left him alone for days when she was partying elsewhere."

"I travel so much that I thought, when the marriage broke up, it would be better for DJ to stay in his own house, near his friends, in the same school," Dan said to me. "He didn't *object* to staying with his mother . . ."

"The D.A. is making a big thing about the fact that Jerry didn't attempt to get into Denver proper from the airport . . ."

"Christ, Pete, there wasn't a taxi at the airport that'd take a chance on the roads . . . and I didn't know then that DJ was at the McPhersons'. Noreen Sue wouldn't let me speak to him but she didn't say it was because he wasn't even in the house."

"And then," Peter gave his friend a disgusted look, "he phoned around, asking friends and enemies about Noreen Sue's activities and DJ's state of mind. All this leads the D.A. to a motive."

177

"The boutique salesgirl remembers selling him the ski jacket and the mask."

"Two masks," I said, "he bought me one because we went out for an invigorating hike Thursday afternoon. I'd bought a ski jacket before Dan did, only I didn't think of needing a mask."

Peter looked questioningly at Dan. "The girl didn't mention selling anything to Jenny."

"Well, she will when she sees me. We talked about the weather and Ireland. But she wouldn't have seen Dan and me together. I had bought the jacket while I was waiting for Dan to join me for lunch. He came in while she was wrapping up my things . . . I got some sweaters and junk, too . . . but he'd forgotten his wallet and gone back to his room for it. She wouldn't have seen us together."

Peter nodded during this explanation.

"I'd forgotten that," Dan said, wearily.

"But definitely and decidedly, Dan was with me from the moment he left Hearty-har-har until the next morning."

"Let's hope the D.A. buys it."

"He'll have to. It's the truth!"

"He'll try to find holes in your statement . . ."

"There aren't any . . ."

Peter gave me a hard, angry look. "He'll try, Jenny. Or he'll try to cast doubt on your personal integrity and morality."

"You mean, if I'd perjure myself because I'm so hard up . . ."

"Shut up, Jenny!" said Dan in a hard voice and he grabbed my hand in a hurtful grasp.

Peter had bounced out of his chair, his face the mask of the worldly attorney.

"I'd better take Jenny back to her hotel."

I got to my feet too, swallowing hard against his decision, scrubbing at my face, and the skin on my head that seemed to be contracting around my brain.

We were all on our feet, tense and upset.

"I'm awfully, awfully tired," I said. "I'd better go while I can still maneuver."

Dan made a move as if to comfort me. That would have been disastrous. I stepped back, saw the uncertainty and shock in Dan's face and forced myself to keep my hands at my sides.

"We can't drop any more stitches now, Dan," I said, trying to soften my apparent rejection. "I'm talked out, wrung out. Please."

He put both hands to his face, rubbing at his temples as if he suffered the same discomfort as I did. But, as his hands came away, he nodded comprehension and swung to the fireplace, leaning his head against the arm he propped on the mantelpiece.

Petra filled the gap with gentle suggestions to me of a hot bath and did I have a tranquillizer? Peter draped my cloak over my shoulders and took my attaché case, though he handed me the knitting bag with a grin and the comment that he'd never live it down if he was seen carrying that. I tried vainly to think of something else to say to Dan to reassure him but I must cultivate a barrier of indifference to him if I had to appear on his behalf in a court, before prying eyes and destructive personalities.

Once Peter settled me in the Buick I shut my eyes and laid my head against the backrest. He was kind enough to keep quiet the entire trip back to the city. He asked me to wait in the car long enough to be sure there were no lingering reporters. In a daze, I signed into the hotel, fumbling in my handbag for my diary. I always write the number of my hotel room down so I can remember it. I couldn't find my diary: it wasn't in my handbag. It wasn't in the attaché case and there was my suitcase on the bellboy's carrier and everyone standing about, waiting for me to finish my rooting.

"What are you looking for, Jenny?"

"My diary." I felt lost without it.

I caught Peter's half grin and remembered. "Oh!" I almost burst into tears. Peter caught my arm firmly and started me to the elevator while I got a grip on myself.

"Remember, Jackson, no phone calls for Dr. Lovell: no visitors no matter how much they pass you!" he said over his shoulder to the reception clerk.

Peter got me to my room, shooed the bellboy out with a second reminder about my privacy, and judging by the grin on the man's face, a hefty tip. Peter pushed me to the bed and on it.

"You won't be disturbed. Sleep yourself out. If you need anything, call my office." He let go of my hands to winkle a card from his wallet which he stuck on the phone dial. "Call me anyway when you wake up. If I'm not there, ask for Barbara."

Still dazed, I heard him leave, fumbling with the doorknob, locking me in.

I sat on the edge of the bed, wanting to cry and unable to. Poor Dan. Poor confused DJ. Then I just kicked off my shoes and struggled under the blankets. I didn't even turn the light off. It was still burning the next morning when I woke up: a shocking waste of energy which, in a much calmer frame of mind, appalled me.

IX

I MADE A SMALL FRONT PAGE HEADLINE, at the bottom, as "Mystery Witness" for D. Jerome Lowell. I was also billed as the well-known lecturer, Doctor Dana Jane Hartman Lovell, BA, MA, PhD, and author of many children's books. There was a recap of the death of Mrs. Noreen Sue Lowell and the arraignment of D. Jerome Lowell on charges of manslaughter.

Depressed by the article, I dutifully phoned Peter's office. He was in and the tone of his greeting did not lift my spirits.

185

"The D.A. still thinks he has a case, Jenny."

"Does that mean I have to hang around Denver?" That did not please me.

"I thought you said your engagements were completed?"

"They are, but I live in Ireland, and I want to see my son."

"You've got one of those excursion tickets?"

"Yes . . ."

"You're not to worry about your expenses," he said firmly.

"They are *not* my main worry. Trials in the States can take ages . . . I want to see my son, he must be worried sick over all this . . . And I have commitments at home . . . in Ireland . . ."

I suppose I sounded petulant. What I feared was that somehow the prurient D.A. would divine that I was in love with Daniel Jerome and that would blow my alibi to flinders. I wanted not to be in Dan's vicinity so that I could keep up my pretense of indifference.

"I can certainly move for an early trial date. But if you did have to go back to Ireland and return here, you're not to worry about your expenses . . ."

"Fuck the expenses," I said with a force and inelegance that made him gasp on the other end. I always save my expletives for emergencies but I chuckled because I had managed to shock Peter Taggert. "You have absolutely no idea how this mucks up my writing schedule. I must have quiet and no interruptions.

186

I can't write when I'm so wound up with worry that creative thought is impossible. I sure as hell-won't-freeze can't write a 'Timmy' story in my present frame of mind. And I've got to. I've a contract to fulfill . . ."

"Jenny, Jenny. Calm down, Jenny. Please listen, Jenny . . ." Peter kept saying as I exploded. "I'll be right over. Call room service and get some food into you. Did you just wake up?"

"Yes, I did. You told me to call you when I woke up. I am."

"Okay, okay. Just order breakfast. Sent up, do you hear? And no reporters. I'll be over in fifteen minutes. I'll probably arrive *with* your breakfast."

The moment I jammed the phone down I was ashamed of my outburst. But I felt better. I'd roared out some of the tension. I ordered a big breakfast from room service. It'd be lunch because my watch read 11:30. I ran a hot, hot bath which revived me, too.

I had just finished dressing when there was a knock on my door. I almost threw it open when caution returned. Leaving the door on the chain, I opened it a bit and asked who was there.

"Bell Captain, Dr. Lovell. Mr. Taggert asked me to give you this when you woke up." The man passed in a thin parcel wrapped in fine white paper. He left before I could tip him.

I unwrapped a leather-bound, gilt-edged slim volume, a diary: much more elegant than my Eason's 50 penny pocket thingie. And in the corner of the front cover, in gold, were my initials: D J H L.

I was astounded and then deeply touched as the pages fell open to yesterday's date. Carefully inscribed in a precise hand were the notations: Arrived Denver, 4:45. See PT, Dinner PT, Hotel Room #804. On today's date was the entry. Lunch PT, discuss DJL case. In the address and phone section all my data had been carefully transcribed in another handwriting. Barbara's, probably, because it was femininely cursive.

And I'd been such a bitch on the phone! I riffled the pages, and smoothed the leather of the binding. I wondered if Peter knew how much Daniel Jerome mattered to me.

Which reminded me. I walked fingers in the yellow pages, found the phone number of the bookstore with the largest ad, called them and asked for three copies of any books they had in stock by Dana Jane Lovell. I asked them to be sent, cash on delivery, to the hotel and the clerk's gasp of surprise when I gave her my name was one of the fringe benefits of being a well-known, or should I say, infamous, person in Denver. If the books arrived in time, I could give them, suitably inscribed, to Peter to deliver to the children.

My brunch and Peter arrived simultaneously. He was ordering some lunch for himself when I made with the door routine.

When I began my enthusiastic thanks for the diary, he tried to brush off the gratitude, telling me to shut up and fill my face. I tried to question him but he said flatly that he never discussed business before breakfast; in this case, mine. He leaned back in his chair and studied a pocket notebook. I was hungry enough to take advantage of this dictum so I plowed through melon, coffee, toast, eggs and sausages until his salad lunch arrived.

"Now," he said, settling before the service table, "I've made some tentative plans for you, subject to your agreement. A petition for an early trial date has been presented in court this morning. I should know the precise date later today. I see no reason why you can't keep to your own plan, and see your son. You were then to have returned to Dublin, right? To work? Can you postpone your commitments in Ireland? I can offer you a ski lodge in Aspen for as long as you require it. Would that give you peace and quiet? I can guarantee you won't be interrupted there."

"Wouldn't the D.A. consider that a bribe?"

"If his bullheadedness requires a material witness to hang around a foreign country, he can't complain about interim accommodations. The least I can do is give a guaranteed retreat until the case is tried so you can get on with your story . . ."

"If I can think of one . . ."

He raised his eyebrows.

"I did mention that my state of mind is not conducive to writing at the moment . . . And I'm not being difficult."

189

"Then visit friends? Relatives? Relax in sunny Florida."

"I'll take the Aspen lodge." I sighed deeply. "What a schmazzle! How's . . . Dan . . . today?"

"Your arrival has given him a new lease on life."

"For a permanent one, you really need the party or parties unknown who did attack his ex-wife."

"Don't I know it. We've not been idle, Jenny, even before you responded. I've got a damned good investigator working. The trouble is, the goddamn blizzard. A car can be seen, a taxi would have had a record, but the wind wiped any tracks to the house, and there were no fingerprints on the windowsills, doorframes . . . She was found in the kitchen, she'd bled to death from a wound in her skull: coroner says the edge of the counter . . ."

"I thought she was in a snow drift . . ."

Peter grimaced. "She was. The back door was open . . ."

"Burglar . . ."

Peter shook his head tolerantly. "A pine tree had come down . . . and through the back door . . ."

"Wasn't she knocked by it?"

"No way. Her body position was wrong, but the snow drifted in."

"Burglar! She discovered him entering because the tree had broken in the back door . . ."

"Possibly and likely though no one has come forward. What points the finger at Jerry is the evidence of a neighbor who saw a man in a ski mask leaving Noreen Sue's house at about ten o'clock. She was watching *Gunga Din* too, and she'd got up to call her dog in. She thought it was odd at the time because there were no lights on in Noreen Sue's house although she says in her statement that there were visitors at all hours to that house."

"Old cow."

"She was horrified to think her evidence might convict that nice Mr. Lowell." Peter's comment chided me for my uncharitable remark. "She said she would not swear it could have been Dan: merely that it was a tall man, wearing a ski mask, ski jacket and pants tucked into boots or ski boots. And that is all she's prepared to swear to."

"And the D.A. can use that sort of flimsy evidence to convict Dan?"

"That is only a part of it."

"Well, it wasn't Dan."

"I believe you!"

"What about those other visitors at all hours?"

He nodded. "We're checking, we're checking but she knew one helluva lot of people who can claim, legitimately, that they were storm-bound. We might just luck out. In the meantime . . ."

"Back at the ranch . . ."

He snorted at my trite attempt at levity. ". . . Jerry's on bail, you're on the spot, and we'll just have to bide our time."

"But I'm telling the truth."

He sighed again for that was equally a cliché.

191

Anne McCaffrey

My package arrived from the bookstore, suspiciously
thin, and as I paid the charges, I realized that I was
going to have to disappoint someone. There were
only two of my books plus a note from the salesgirl
apologizing and saying that she'd special order the
others. She'd tried to phone me at the hotel but had
been unable to reach me. Would I please ring her?

"Please explain to Pierrot and Alexandra that I
could only get these copies. I'll send them each a
set . . ."

"There's no need . . ."

"I don't disappoint my fans. . . . My publisher can
mail them." I was inscribing the books, one to the two
girls and the other to DJ, "Otherwise you'll have
squabbles and that would defeat my purpose."

"Now, what do you want to do next? Visit with
your son?"

"Yes."

"Then, come back to Denver and what will you
need in the lodge?"

I gave him a sideways look, then sighed and got
sensible. "Plenty of typing paper, an electric typewriter if possible; is the place within walking distance
of a shop?"

"All supplies will be laid in, there's a phone,
plenty of oil, plenty of firewood. Do you ski? Oh,
well."

"Mail?"

"Have it forwarded to my office, I'll see you get it
without delay."

192

"Helicopter or trusty sledge-dog?"

He grinned, merely assuring me all would be taken care of. Then he rose, held my hand in a very tight grip to signify his friendship and appreciation and left me with the final warning to keep to my room. I'd be driven to the airport tomorrow morning.

I was content with that and watched TV, deliberately worried at the pattern of a new sweater. I think I undid the first two rows five times before I got all the bobbles in place and the ocean wave pattern correctly spaced. That kept me from thinking about other things.

Petra drove me to the airport the next morning because Peter was so frightfully busy and a reporter was hanging about his office. Alexandra and Pierrot were thrilled with my book and the inscription. DJ had gone into space and stayed in his room so she assumed that he was equally delighted if less volatile. She worried about the weather because it was snowing lightly again and they'd had so many snowdays already this year. Not only was school work suffering but it was so hard to keep the kids from breaking their necks on the slopes behind the house. She refused to take them to the hills if they were out of school due to snow. Her chatter was soothing, normal, recounted in a humorous tone with great good nature. I didn't have to do more than make occasional noises.

At the airport I wouldn't let her wait with me for my plane. The snow was descending with more determination so she didn't argue.

193

"I'll see you soon, Petra, and thank Peter for everything. Especially my new 'brains.' "

She regarded me blankly until I waved the diary.

"Your 'brains' are saving Jerry's neck. And he told me to tell you to keep all your stitches on your needles."

Well, a crumb is better than nothing.

When I handed the clerk my ticket, she made me out another new one, with an open return for Denver. I sat in the proper lounge by the correct gate, watching the snow fall down; alternately wishing the plane wouldn't be able to take off and that nothing would delay me now.

I really shouldn't have rented a car for the drive from Philadelphia to Bethlehem but I knew the road and it was the quickest way to Tim and his sanity. I called him from Friendship Airport and arranged for him to book me a room at the hotel and meet me there. I haven't done that much lefthand driving in ages and I had a couple of near misses which made me take it more slowly than my usual slap-dash Irish driving style. When I arrived Tim was pacing the hotel lobby, for all the world like his father, and his bear hug of relief all but cracked my ribs.

He started issuing orders to the clerk and the bellgirl in her short skirt and high white boots. Before I could protest, my luggage was whisked away and I was in the bar with a drink in my hand and Tim coping with everything. We had a quiet dinner and a few more drinks. He wouldn't let me talk. He wined, dined and deposited me in bed with a capsule to make me sleep like "right now." He gave me a lovely hug and a kiss and patted me on the head. I went to sleep blessing my good fortune in sons, and not for the first time.

The sleep revived me and I met Tim at the University Center and had a snack lunch with him. He then conned me into visiting the book store and into buying a Texas Instrument SR-50 which he said he needed to speed up his physics homework which was brutal. I had to listen to his explanation about the various functions, memory, places until I reminded him that even slide rules defeated me. I was a librarian, not a mathematician. He went on to his afternoon classes, with a cocky step for his chicanery, and I got myself a hair appointment which did my morale a lot of good.

I phoned my publishers in the afternoon about the books and was promised instant shipment. I talked with the lecture bureau and they'd had good reports but we agreed that my schedule had been very stiff and that next year's would be arranged with more regard for breathing spaces. I did not mention the case to them but I did to my agent. As I expected, Sam remarked that all publicity was useful but could I please make a practice of avoiding any future mur . . . sorry, manslaughter suspects?

The five o'clock news on TV brought the good word that the Midwest was again blanketed in snow. I'd got out of Denver in good time.

At dinner I gave Tim the whole story of my involve-

195

ment with manslaughter. I emphasized that distinction. I didn't tell Tim the *whole* story, but Tim was not naïve and I wanted him to know that I had a very good opinion of Daniel Jerome despite his circumstantial guilt. I could quite understand why Tim might be jaundiced about a man who'd got his mother messed up in a mur . . . manslaughter charge. Tim swore at women like Noreen Sue who'd neglect a child. Tim was gripping my hand firmly at that point and I looked up with throat-jamming gratitude at the bony broad shoulders of my offspring, the strong but unmarked face and the keen eyes behind the glasses. I'd made enough money to afford contact lenses for him and the glasses hid his best feature, very clear green eyes, but he kept wanting useful things like microscopes and telescopes and SR-50s.

Now that my budget of news was over, I realized that he had something of moment to tell me. "She" was a Cedar Crest student, with a really lovely singing voice who didn't mind that he couldn't carry a tune so long as he knew how to *appreciate* decent music. Her name was Patricia Newlands and her nickname was Trish. Would I be staying long enough in town to meet her or did I have to fly back to Denver right away? The next day was Saturday and he had no classes but she did until one. Would I like to meet her?

I had some difficulty remaining calm, cool and collected I was so pleased. Tim, wrapped up in what

196

was his first serious girl, mistook my dignity for hurt feelings.

"Hey, Mom, you'll always be my best girl. You don't have to worry."

"Not now, I don't."

"Huh? You weren't worried about me, were you?"

In point of fact, I had had several twinges. I was absolutely certain Tim was completely masculine but we'd had such a close relationship, such a fine understanding, that I had had some misgivings about dominant female-mothers and lack of male-father-figures and that sort of go-round. At the time when I thought he should be going with one girl, he was still part of his special group of boy friends who seemed to date a corresponding group of girl friends. Tim had seemed to specialize in giving considered advice to both girls and boys as if being an American, with an American mother, gave him special insight. Which it probably did since sex education in Ireland is a no-no.

"Well . . ." I began, temporizing.

"Mom!" Tim was shocked, annoyed, disappointed and disgusted.

"Well, I tried not to be the heavy mother . . ."

"Ah, no way, Mom. It's just, well . . . I didn't find someone I felt you'd like. . . . You knew all the girls in Blackrock. And I always had someone about . . ."

I was properly abashed and asked about Trish. I had built one picture which dissolved the moment I met Trish in the flesh the next day. She was exceed-

197

ingly feminine (Tim had said she could cycle all day without complaining), with close cropped black curls (natural, Tim had told me) and an "interesting" face. (I am not being snide but Trish had the type of looks which mature, not a transient prettiness that so often fades into discontent in an older personality.) She was so lively, so natural that you forgot her appearance in the glow of her warm merriness.

Tim had brought his guitar (he can't sing but he does play) and when he asked her to sing for me in the hotel room, she obliged without simpering disclaimers. She asked me what sort of songs I liked best and, when Tim said I was a folk song freak, she sang several which Joan Baez had made popular. She had a lovely voice, warm and true and though she didn't need much volume to carry in the hotel room, I sensed a strength. Certainly she sounded better than some of the singers I'd endured recently on TV programs.

We had dinner and she told me that she had no intentions of settling down but she rather doubted her chances of making a name for herself. She'd be quite happy to find a good church or school job since such employment was secure and she liked working with children and chorale groups. Musical training was an ace in the hole, she felt, and it was so "iffy" to set your sights on the Met or City Center when there were so many other satisfying careers available in music.

Inadvertently I found myself comparing Trish with

my young nephew's Linda: and Sam with Tim. Then I decided that there was no comparison in temperament and character. And none, I hoped, in situation.

As I drove the car to Cedar Crest to get Trish in on time, she asked me if I'd like to listen to the school church choir the next morning.

"Mom's very tired, Trish," Tim said hastily, knowing how I felt about organized religions.

"I should have thought of that, Mrs. Lovell. Tim told me what a heavy schedule you've had. How many miles in how many days?"

"Tim can figure it out on the SR-50."

"I'm awfully glad I had a chance to meet you, Mrs. Lovell, without having to come all the way to Ireland, that is." She gave Tim a look and then thanked me again for dinner. I wished her luck and turned the car about as Tim walked her to the dormitory door.

Tim had something on his mind when he got back into the car but I didn't question him. I didn't want to answer any more and if he had something to say, I knew of old that it'd come out when he felt the time was right. The Denver business obviously upset him and he had obviously not mentioned it to Trish. He kissed me good night when I delivered him to his dorm door and warned me to drive home carefully, to sleep late and he'd phone around noontime.

I was pleasantly tired when I parked the car in the hotel lot. However, no sooner had I got settled in bed and closed my eyes, than the old brain spun 'round and 'round. I wished I'd asked Tim for another capsule.

Generally I do a lot of constructive thinking on my insomniac nights: it's the only way to cope with them. In my own home, I'm apt to get up and go to the typewriter and see what'll happen. Here I tossed and turned, wrestling with the problems of returning to Denver and all that could happen nasty.

I envisioned myself superbly poised while the D.A. ruthlessly cross-examined me with all the rapier wit and studied contempt of the TV prototype. I, like the sauve polished barrister of JUSTICE, a veritable Margaret Lockwood in bag wig, replied with cool candour and resilience. I thought up ninety-two euphemisms for *not* admitting Dan and I had had sexual relations. Then my errant mind reviewed those passages at arms.

Nothing turns me off quicker than the mawkish sight of a middle-aged woman besotted with a younger man. Daniel Jerome was 42, so he wasn't that much younger than I. But 42 does not look up the scale towards 50; he roguishly turns his eyes down to the 30s or the 20s or if he's a damned fool, the late teens.

Besides the age factor, I was inextricably linked with what was probably one of the most unpleasant periods of his life. I couldn't imagine him wanting a permanent reminder. What had we in common, besides a son apiece, a wacky sense of humor, twenty laps of a pool before puffing, and, I sighed fretfully, a rather unusual sexual rapport.

That happy sympathy had been compounded by the romantic situation of snow-boundery, appetite and opportunity. At that point, not only was I handy and agreeable, I probably struck him (an image I generally present) as a sensible woman, quite unlikely to cause scenes and raise hell if disappointed/dismissed/disillusioned. I had also been, at the moment of our bedding, completely divorced from his situation—which he had taken pains not to discuss with me—and therefore impartial and impersonal.

Everyone has moments they wish to savor again and again. And the pleasure, the sense of superb well-being that I'd savored that Thursday, that fateful Thursday night watching TV . . .

I sat upright. TV. I got out of bed and turned on the set provided by the management. At least, in the States, you had night long TV to distract the insomniac. Firmly I concentrated on some ancient, now creaking but occasionally enjoyable Melvyn Douglas situation comedy. I even managed to fall asleep with the thing winking and shifting light patterns all night long.

The early news advised me that the Midwest was still storm-bound. Pennsylvania was demonstrably bright and sunny with seasonably mild temperatures. I shut the TV off and dozed for another hour and a half. I still had time to kill before Tim's call so I breakfasted downstairs in the hotel dining room. Then I wandered about scenic restored colonial Bethlehem. I could wish that other cities had executed their urban renewals with as much thought and care. Before I'd

201

visited Tim's university, I'd had a mental picture of the great steel foundries burping noxious gases into the air and a vista of a dank, horrible industrial town. Bethlehem, with a Christmas star hidden on its dominating slope, was refreshing.

I ran up the mileage on the rented car while Tim and I toured Allentown for a place to lunch. We discussed at length his courses for the coming year. He intended to return to Ireland as soon as his last final exam was over. Would I ask Mr. Hengarty, our landlord, if Tim could have his usual summer job, but starting July 1st.

"I thought I'd take June off as a holiday this year. You know, kinda hack around with the others."

"You do that anyway, if I can get you out of bed."

"You know, I was thinking, what with people asking me questions I couldn't answer, that I don't know that much about Ireland, except Wicklow and Dublin. And that's the other thing, would you have the Raleigh people check my bike over? And my bike pack needs a new strap."

I dutifully took out my diary and made the appropriate notations.

"Hey, is that the one you got in place of your evidence?"

I let him look, pointing smugly to the gilt initials. I didn't realize it then but Tim had adroitly changed the subject on me.

"Say, how long would that sort of thing take?"

"If you mean until your last exam in May, I sin-

202

cerely hope not. Peter Taggert said he was going to file for an early trial date . . ."

"Early next year?"

I hardly thought so but the possibility was a nagging worry. If they were willing to pay my expenses and air fare to and from Denver, they could bloody extend the benefit to Ireland and let me work where I was comfortable. I felt shrewish and berated myself for such unworthy thoughts. Fortunately it was now time to collect Trish from Cedar Crest as her duties with the college choir were over.

Trish and Tim were both as relaxed with me as gooseberry that day. It was bright sunny weather so we went for a drive, to the Pennsylvania Dutch area. Corny, but it gets me to drive through small towns called Intercourse, Bird of Paradise and King of Prussia. We noticed the signs of storm damage, trees down, barns with roofs half torn off and Tim and Trish regaled me about the hurricane force winds in early April. We tried to persuade Trish that Ireland is a windy place, too, with winds regularly at gale force 6 and 8.

This afternoon it was obvious to me, the two being unable to hide their affection, that Tim and Trish were very much attached to each other. Tim sat between us in the front seat of the car, with an arm impartially about both "girls," but I noticed that his hand curled around her shoulder. Which is as it should be. We found a restaurant which boasted seven sweets and seven sours, and made pigs of ourselves. I should never eat dumplings. I had indigestion all the way back and couldn't wait to drop the two of them off so I could get on the outside of an alkalizer.

By Monday morning, I was feeling rested, restless and resentful of the circumstances which prevented my returning home. There was not much to do in Bethlehem with Tim, and Trish, in classes. I could spend only so much time browsing in shops in the city center or admiring the historical exhibits. I could go over to New York and pester my sister but it meant sleeping in the same room with Veronica. I'd already spent three days with her at the start of my tour when I was doing my publishers and agent.

I considered, at breakfast, phoning my friend, Mairead, in Ireland. She was staying in the cottage, feeding the dog, and house-sitting. She'd be at the boutique at this hour but a call would be full rate. Natural instincts of economy intervened. Similar instincts kept me from doing more than window-shopping but I managed to waste most of the morning.

When I got back to the hotel from my aimless time-killing, there was a message for me to call a Denver number, collect.

It was Peter. At his jovial greeting, my midsection went into a state of spasm from anticipation.

"The news is A-okay, all systems go. We did it. We got Jerry off without a trial. Charges are completely dropped. Guess why?"

"Well, the news said you had another blizzard.

Did you have an epidemic of house burglars in ski masks?''

"How the hell did you guess?"

"How do you think I write children's books? What actually happened?"

"Two clowns were apprehended in the act. They were wearing ski masks and one was tall enough to be Mrs. Gresham's snowman. But,'' and Peter paused to emphasize the point, "when his apartment was searched, items were found which had been stolen the night of the first blizzard from houses not far from Noreen Sue's.''

"Huh! Isn't that circumstantial evidence, too?"

"Whose side are you on?" Peter sounded surprised at my remark. "It's enough for me to blow Mathews' set of circumstances. That and you."

"I thought you thought he wouldn't buy my alibi?"

Peter chuckled, a smug, self-satisfied legal laugh. "I have it on good authority he was already unhappy."

"Oh?" Peter had a goodie to tell me and wanted to take his own time.

"You see, his daughter goes to the same school my girls attend. When Laura found out that 'Timmy's' author was vouching for Mr. Lowell, she told Pierrot that she was going to tell Daddy a thing or two."

While the scene so conjured had tremendous dramatic possibilities, I didn't quite see a ten-year-old daughter dissuading a father from pressing a manslaughter charge. Admittedly American youngsters have a great deal more freedom than Irish kids but . . .

205

"You don't mean that the nasty D.A. was persuaded by his daughter?"

"No," the reply was firm, "but you'll remember I said that he would try to weaken your testimony by a smear campaign? I think he realized that your integrity is well-nigh unassailable, Dr. Lovell. And the circumstantial evidence of the ski-masked burglars gives us all an out."

"Us all? What do you mean? I was telling the truth. That should have counted for more than my title or the fortuitous greed of thieves."

"No," said Peter slowly, thoughtfully, "we don't like to say such things in books for our children, do we? But it exists and is a viable force in modern, polite, sophisticated society." He gave a rueful laugh. "I wish you did have to come back to Denver, Jenny. It was a real pleasure to meet you and not just because you were ready and willing to lay your reputation on the line to help Jerry . . ."

I was glad he hadn't read my mind of the previous evening or this morning.

". . . and Petra and the girls will be mighty disappointed too."

I wanted to ask if Dan would be. Instead, I said, "Please tell Dan how tremendously relieved I am that he's been cleared of the charge. And . . . and tell DJ, and the girls, that I asked my publisher to send them . . ."

"You don't have to do that, Jenny."

"I've done it. I never disappoint my fans, Peter."

206

"I don't think you could."

The ring in his voice embarrassed me and I stammered something, remembering to mention the diary, and how elegant it was and how kind of him.

"I'll send yours back to you. Are you returning to Ireland right away?"

I really didn't know and said so. "Remember me to Dan," I said, which was as inane as it was inadequate.

"He's not likely to forget you, Jenny," Peter said and then, with a formal phrase of thanks and goodbye, rang off.

How anti-climactic! How bloody depressing! Not that I wasn't overwhelmingly pleased that Dan, and I, were vindicated: that he was spared the stigma of a trial and DJ more crushing uncertainty. The truth had out! We had told it but the irony was it wasn't the truth that had made Dan free! It was lucking out with the ski-masked burglars: pure chance.

And I was expected to go back and write children's books? Full of high moral integrity and ideals like Truth, Honesty, Kindness? Were my 'Timmy' tales *really* what I should be telling youngsters? Or the unvarnished truth of adult life that was facing them? And yet, the Good Guys had won this round *because* my reputation was good: and the principles I stood for in my books had tipped the creaky scales of Justice for a nice guy in the clutch of circumstance.

My mood was composed of many elements, few of them complimentary to the shining image that had

207

helped reprieve Dan. I think I felt cheated that my "sacrifice" was not needed. I knew I was damned sorry I wasn't going to see Dan, under whatever circumstances, again. And I wanted to see his son, too, to see the boy no longer haunted but happy the way boys should be . . . before they have to grow up. I worried that I had raised Tim right, if my sojourn in Denver were an example of what he might face. I was disoriented, too, because I'd just geared myself to working elsewhere other than my home when I must suddenly switch again. Mostly I couldn't wait to get myself on a plane and back to Ireland, to what was familiar, unexceptional, anonymous and dull. I yearned to be "missus" and talk of the weather and hear complaints about the desperate prices of food, the high rates and the "turrible inconveniences of the latest strike." To get away from the sleek look of hotel rooms and effusive p.r. men and babbling do-gooders and idiotic ideals.

I got on the phone to Aer Lingus and booked myself on a flight that evening. If I pushed myself, I could make it and still have a few hours with Tim. Once I make up my mind . . .

I could leave packing till after my lunch with Tim. He was genuinely relieved that the charges against Dan had been dropped. He might have been proud of my sense of obligation but he hadn't liked his mother involved in a "hairy" situation. I think, under other circumstances, Tim would have liked Dan.

We went to the Maples for lunch because I was a

208

bit bored with the hotel food. We'd finished the shrimp cocktails when Tim got round to what I had sensed must have been on his mind for some time.

"Mom," he began in the casual tone of someone who has spent hours rehearsing, "if Trish wangled a plane ticket out of her old man, do you think she could visit us in Ireland a while this summer? She's saved enough to keep her while she's there . . ."

"I can't see why not," I said, keeping my face straight with an effort and matching his diffidence.

"Then you liked her?" There was a little leaping of gladness in his eyes.

"Of course, I liked her." I damned the Denver affair again for my preoccupation with it. I ought to have seen how important Trish was to Tim. "She's got a lovely voice, plays beautifully, and she's got her head on right. If you'd like, I'll make a formal invitation to her parents . . ."

"Ah, Mom, no one does that anymore."

"I do. If I had a daughter . . ."

His eyebrows went up and he regarded me with all the amused tolerance of the young generation for the vagaries of the older. I plowed on.

"Her parents are much more likely to cough up for that all important ticket if the invitation comes from me. You know your generation but I sure as hell know mine. And it's very obvious to me that Trish comes from a 'good' family and is very well brought up."

We thrashed that topic about a while and it ended

209

that I would write the invitation for him to give Trish for her parents . . . as a clincher.

There was more to her proposed trip to Ireland than vacationing. She wanted to research the Irish musical form called lilting, or lumming, in which the singer mouths syllables instead of words to the music of drum, accordion or fiddle. I'd heard it with Tim when he went to Kerry one Easter. I suppose the form had academic merit. I couldn't, however, imagine Trish wasting her lovely voice on lilting. Would that have occurred to her as a research subject before she met Tim? Ah, the resourcefulness of the young is awesome. I was touched, amused and delighted with the pair of them.

And suddenly very envious.

We finished lunch in a welter of enthusiastic plans and I used three pages of my new diary to make preparation notes. I was to check the tent and see if we needed new pegs or lines: Trish had her own sleeping bag. (Did I dare ask Tim how he knew?) Would I ask Eamonn Dunne if we could have the loan of his sister's bike? Tim was going to lay in a supply from that great store in Philadelphia which specialized in dehydrated and flash frozen camper foods. The questions and queries were still coming thick and fast when I dropped him back to the campus for his afternoon lab.

He stroked my hair as he often does in farewell, boyishly awkward, more as if he were caressing a dog than his mother. (There are certain things a mother *can't* instruct her son in but I rather hoped he was more adroit with Trish.) Then he gave me a quick, absentminded kiss and, wishing me a safe journey home, went off to class. Already he was thinking ahead: I could tell that in his jaunty step, the tilt of his head. He reminded me so of his six-year-old self, saying a nonchalant goodbye to Mommie on his first day of school.

I got back to my hotel room, called the cashier to ready my bill and shoved my clothes back in the case. When I came to my knitting bag, I spread the finished Arran sweater in my lap. I carefully refolded it and then sat, thinking, thinking of snow, and love-making, and Daniel Jerome Lowell, and the *good* things which had occurred in Denver. I hadn't knitted the sweater with him in mind nor had I finished it as a gift for him but unquestionably he'd look good in it with his broad shoulders. It would cover that incipient midriff roll . . . unless he'd swum it off. Or worried it away. If he intended to live in Denver for DJ's sake, he'd need the thick warm oiled wool . . . in snowstormy Colorado.

The desk clerk was surprised at my request but before I could fret, he sent the bellgirl up with a used, but good, length of wrapping paper and a ball of twine. So I packaged the sweater and addressed it to D.J. Lowell, c/o Peter Taggert. I chuckled and put my initials and Tim's college box number as return address. Then I slipped the unused portion of the Denver ticket into an envelope to mail back to Peter.

He oughtn't to have any trouble getting the refund since his office had paid for it.

I was keyed up now and got on the road to New York, and Ireland, by mid-afternoon. I'd mail the sweater from the airport. Cost me less and give me something to do while I waited for the nine o'clock flight. I didn't miss all the commuter traffic out of New York City but then I did have time to kill. When I had paid the rental car fee, I wondered if it wouldn't have been cheaper to have flown from Philadelphia. But the activity of driving had been therapeutic . . . if expensive.

I phoned my agent to tell him the news, asked him to check to make sure the books had been sent. I dutifully called Suzie and said that, unfortunately, I wouldn't get a chance to see her because my excursion time had run out. She kept yattering on about her husband and the price of meat and this and that until my coins dropped into the box and released me from the sound of her carping. I promised I'd write her and we were cut off. I mailed Dan the sweater.

I needed a drink. I had three, and two dishes of salted peanuts. I organized my documents, including sales slips as I was *not* going to go through last year's fracas with your friendly, alert, penny-pinching, peel-paring, petty-pawed excise officials.

Two guys tried to pick me up: the light in the bar was bad or they'd've seen I was old enough to be their mother. I must have presented them a challenge because I didn't encourage them in spite of the fact that the sun was shining, the forecast clear, and there was no likelihood that I'd be grounded in New York. Once bit, twice shy. They did buy me another drink.

I recall boarding the damned plane, but that's all. Midweek, off-season, the passengers were almost outnumbered by staff and the entire mid-section of the Jumbo was unused. I got a blanket and a pillow or two from the stewardess, fixed the armrests and curled up for sleep. I missed my in-flight dinner, but I really slept. I only woke when the stewardess roused me with juice, coffee and roll.

But Ireland was under the wings and I felt relieved and rested.

Mairead's car was *not* in the blacktopped parking slot in front of the house so she was at work. She kept erratic hours and I hadn't told her when I'd be returning, but it is flat to come home to an empty place. My battered green Peugeot 404 was tucked in by the fuschia hedge, looking dustier than ever with rain splotches. As I paid off the taxi, (my last extravagance for a long while) I hoped that the Peug's battery was okay. Mairead had promised to use the car enough to keep it running.

Baggins came charging out of nowhere, white-tipped black-tail threatening to wind off his tailbone in his ecstasy at seeing me. Where had I been so long? So glad I was home, lick-lick, bark-bark, getting under my feet, impeding my progress up the front stairs. I gave up at his importunities, knelt and accepted the one lick-kiss which he felt his due, then he wiggle-waggled and barged at me with body and nose to reassure me of his welcome all over again. I wonder if the Irish had a dog in mind when they say "cead mille failte"—a thousand welcomes. A dog certainly tries.

The house had the still, un-lived-in quality, airless and dry, but clean. Mrs. Munday who comes to me on Tuesday had not evidently come to do her weekly good-turn. I like to come home to a clean house, but a very tidy one makes me uncomfortable for some obscure reason. My room, when I lugged my growing-heavier-with-every-step case up the stairs, looked unfamiliar, austere and depressing. I'd tidied everything before I left, so that the desk, bare of my usual novelistic clutter, looked more accusatory than clean. There was a neat pile of letters in all sizes and types of envelopes: quite a few airmails and air letters, too, and some half dozen manila envelopes and a couple of book mailers. I sighed: too much too soon. I like my mail in small doses so I can savor it with the second cup of coffee. Generally speaking my first daily contact with the world is Mr. Murphy, the bike-pedalling mailman, resembling, but better looking than, Barry Fitzgerald.

I opened the meadow window and breathed in the crisp cool air: Ireland was its misty self, but the grass was brilliant green, dotted here and there with early weed flowers, white, pinkish and tiny blue stars. The room began to breathe again, too, coming alive with my return and clutter. I opened the mountain window, but my usual view was obscured by the 'soft' weather. I must have stood looking out the window in thanksgiving for some while. The bleat of a motorist on the winding road outside my oasis penetrated my abstraction. I threw off my cloak, opened my case which I hadn't relocked after customs (the man had passed me with no more than a glance at my carefully annotated figures) and I hauled out all the washables. I shucked out of the clothes I'd travelled in, including the underthings, found a fresh change from my drawers and closets. I'd bathe later when the water was hot enough: right now just the change made me feel less sticky. Trailing laddered panty hose and dirty jerseys, I clumped downstairs to the kitchen and stuffed the washing machine with the first load. The lingerie could dry by the fire, the other things on the line if the sun stayed out.

The refrigerator was not full: what was available did not tempt my appetite. The freezer's contents were likewise unappealing, and unidentifiable. I'd better shop for immediate foodstuffs. Mairead hated to cook and would exist for months on a diet of fried eggs, sausages and mash. She would even descend to using packaged potatoes, an anathema to me. I made myself coffee, using the last of the milk in the fridge. Mairead also had a thing about putting out milk bottles and there were a dozen waiting to be returned. Important things like a full bowl of fresh water for

215

Baggins, plenty of canned and dried food for him, had not been neglected.

From the window over the kitchen sink I could survey my kitchen garden. My lettuces were thriving, the beets and carrots sprouting with vigor, the onion sets rising from the ground with green spires. By the walk, last year's glads were piercing the moist dirt which had been weeded, and the roses were pruned and ruddy-leaved with new growth.

And in Colorado, the snows were drifted deep and thick. . . . And, I added briskly, in Pennsylvania they still had that brown stuff that grass turned into in a stateside eastcoast winter.

How glad Tim would be to return to green Ireland! As glad as I was? Or was I?

I found my jacket, my car keys, raced upstairs to retrieve my purse and left my home. The car started, the chain rattling comfortably. I'd often wondered in whimsy if ghost chains sounded at all like a Peugeot's inner workings.

And so I picked up the threads of my Irish life, about where I'd left it six weeks before when I'd gone blithely off on my tour.

But I wasn't the same person.

My friend, Mairead, arrived home from her boutique at 6:15, utterly knackered as she was prone to say.

"You're back early," she remarked, standing in the doorway and glowering at me where I sat going through the mail pile. "Whyn't you let a person know?

216

Christ, I could have closed the shop." Which she did
at the drop of a hat. Mairead has really red hair, she
walks as if her bones might fall away from the joints
at any moment, because she had no meat on her at
all. She believes in nobody and nothing, argues with
me on every topic imaginable so that it is surprising
our friendship survives; she derides my philosophy
and theories, reads all my books in manuscript and
print and consistently reserves her judgment, remaining in her aloof way my closest and most valued
friend. "You didn't think to bring in any Carlsburg?"

"Yes, I noticed you'd drunk it all," and as she
sagged into the couch, I rose to refill my own and get
one for her.

"Ah, that reaches those unrefreshed places," she
said, swigging down half the glass.

She did look exhausted, dark smudges under her
darker eyes. Her hand was shaking a bit and I suspected that Mairead hadn't been eating properly again.
She not only manages the boutique, but does the
buying of European giftie-type thingies twice or three
times a year.

"How'd it go, pet?" she asked me, meaning the
trip.

"Great," I replied with an equal lack of enthusiasm.

"Oh, like that, huh? I told you I thought they
wouldn't pay you just for talking."

I laughed. That had been one of her arguments:
who would pay someone for just talking?

217

"Oh, I got paid. As soon as I stopped talking, my hand went out for the cheque."

She raised her eyebrows, mockingly. "Well, well. And did you see my boyfriend?"

Mairead is genuinely fond of Tim: they have a running battle of insults, digs, innuendoes and arguments which get extremely heated at times, occasionally to the point of my frantic intervention. So I told her about my visits with Tim, and about Trish and her research on lilting.

"Is that what the young call *it* this generation?" she asked with one skeptical eyebrow raised.

Tim says that Mairead speaks better body than Queen's English, using the various parts of her anatomy to express the impressions and feelings she does well not to express verbally.

"Hope she's good enough for him! Are you willing to resign in her favor?"

That was another of her favorite arguments: overmothering the young. That all kids would turn out better if deprived of doting mamas at an early age. As Mairead had been an abandoned child, I would have thought she'd feel quite the opposite.

"I don't think it's come to that, but he is seriously taken with the girl and she is a very nice child."

"Have they, do you think?"

"I don't know and I haven't thought."

"Now, now, mother dear, don't get huffy with me."

"For God's sake, Mairead, what they do is their own business."

"I'll remind you of that one day, pet."

I caught hold of my temper because sometimes Mairead says outrageous things and I never know if she means them or is merely having me on. "I'm sure you wouldn't forget to, Mairead." I felt that now was the time to shut her up with the gifties I'd procured in the States. Last year I'd brought her back a body-shirt and she'd complained bitterly that I'd only brought her the one because it was the most useful garment she'd ever worn.

This year I brought six, bought in various parts of the country, wherever the sales were tempting. She was unreservedly overjoyed with my selections. Then she made me show her the things I'd bought myself and, although I tried to be casual about the ski jacket and mask, and the sweater, she is very perceptive. I avoided the issue by cooking dinner, chattering on about places and people, all the while aware that she suspected I was leaving something of great moment out.

Then I wondered why I was withholding the story from her—I wouldn't have to draw diagrams to Mairead—but she'd certainly hoot over the manslaughter charge and my part in fouling up the D.A.'s case. I could hear her chortling with glee when she learned that my 'reputation' in Denver, at least, was unassailable. It was obvious that my brief affair with Dan meant more to me, much more to me, than to parade it for amusement before my friend, even though she was my best friend.

She didn't press me, knowing that eventually I'd come out with it in my own good time. She told me her own news: surprisingly good sales at Easter, a good contract with a 'reliable' firm in the States wanting to be supplied with handknits, though shipping costs were triple what they'd been three years ago. I still had that feeling of disorientation you get when you realize that life has continued in its usual merry pace despite your absence.

She didn't, however, spend the final night at my house but, after dinner, packed her things with such alacrity that I suspected she had a boyfriend again. She insisted house and Baggins had been no trouble, she'd do it again, so long as I continued to provide her with body-shirts.

I don't get as de-synchronized travelling east as I do going west. I had no trouble getting to sleep that night.

The next morning I struck off in my usual routine, rising at eight to let my eager Baggins out for his morning tour of duty and inspection. I had one cup of coffee waiting for the mail, another reading the Alumnae Bulletin, the sole piece of morning mail. I dutifully went upstairs to write thank-you notes for hospitality but here the routine dribbled away.

As I stared out the window, I had to admit to myself that routine was not going to suffice me. Distance had not ended my attachment to Dan-the-

Man. Had our romantic interlude ended after that snowstorm, I think I could have talked myself out of the infatuation. But I'd had to go to his rescue and when you put yourself on the line for someone, like the Chinese adage, you become irretrievably involved. I hadn't saved Dan's life as had been claimed but I had saved him from the ignominy of standing trial and a possible twenty year sentence for manslaughter. Okay, to split a semantic hair, I suppose I had saved him the better part of his active life. He'd have been 60-ish when he got out—if they'd been able to make that asinine charge stick. I found myself wishing the bondage were more than Chinesely proverbial but I had also done my living best to keep it nebulous. I pondered now on the folly of sending him that sweater. But the deed was done and couldn't be undone, excepting postal inefficiencies. I was glad I had done it, and told myself to expect nothing in return for the gesture. Such ruminations were not making bread and butter come in, nor writing those thank-yous.

My mother, bless her heart, had a thing about discipline: you disciplined your mind and your body, and I always flung back at her, your heart. That wasn't precisely true, or fair. And I only learned what she meant during Ray's illness. Particularly about disciplining the heart—in my case, not to break while I watched him waste away and die.

So I set about exercising discipline. I tried not to see resemblances to Dan in strangers who just happened to have silvery hair and bushy moustaches,

were the same height and general build. I succeeded
in that endeavor in the next few weeks. What I couldn't
succeed in bending to my will was my memory of
smell, curiously enough. It seemed to me that in the
April crispness of County Wicklow I could scent the
Denver air, crisp with snow and cold and pine, min-
gled with those indefinable evocative scents of ironed
cotton, maleness and aftershave lotion. I was also
physically ill with wanting to feel his hands on me,
his lips on mine, the prickle of his moustache against
my nose and lips, the water smoothness of his flesh
against mine. I bloody woke up a couple of nights
whimpering in my sleep for that reassurance. And
wished him the same sort of frustration, damning his
luck that, as a man he had more chance of easing his
condition than I.

Some of my frustration also stemmed from the
realization that Tim had found himself a female
companion. Not usurping my place in his affections,
God forbid, but Tim maturing enough to stretch past
our rewarding relationship to attach himself to a nu-
bile female. I had never been a possessive or clinging
female. I wouldn't start now, if I had to tie mental
and literal hands behind my back and gag my mouth.
I wanted for Tim what Ray and I had enjoyed before
he got sick. My respect, admiration and deep love for
Raymond Lovell had sustained me through the adjustment after his death and my loneliness while Tim was
growing up. But I saw more loneliness ahead of me
as Tim graduated from the position of 'man in my

life.' Trish was helping to write on that particular wall in my emotional life and I'd better start planning ahead.

I don't like solitary living. I had had to discipline myself to accept Tim's departure to University but I could look forward to his summer return. I would have less of his time this year, and, God willing, still less of it from now on. Which was as it should be, but what did I do with the emptiness his going left? I thought of Beth, with Sam and Linda producing a grandchild to fill her lonely hours. I never had been especially maternal: Tim and I were more friends, than son and mother. That flexibility would be a help but . . . there ain't no all night TV in Ireland. Discipline included occupation, and while I didn't wear a hair shirt, I knitted hairy Arrans. I finished a size 42 sweater, which usually takes a good fortnight, in less than nine days.

Mairead had also made herself scarce in my company: at first I thought she'd had enough of the lodge. Then I began to worry if I'd said something that had irritated her. She took umbrage at the most unlikely things. I finally realized that she must be in the throes of a new love affair and I'd better discipline myself out of such subjective whimsies.

When I brought the finished Arran in to her boutique, her reaction substantiated my guess. She was looking extremely well, with a certain smugness in her manner and a warmth in her eyes. She was as sharp-tongued as ever as she took the sweater and began folding it to display in a plastic cover.

"You just brought one in . . . about ten days ago. Don't tell me you did a 42 in. . . . Well, who is he?" We were alone in the shop but she glanced around anyhow. "Anybody I know?"

I shook my head.

"Ah, c'mon, Dana. Who is it?"

"When I was in the States . . ."

"You do pick 'em," she said with an exaggerated sigh of disgust. "Go on . . ."

"I got grounded in Denver by a blizzard."

"I remember the late news about unseasonable blizzards but then the weather everywhere this year had been unreal. So, tell me . . ."

"All planes were grounded . . ."

"Him, too . . ."

"And so the airlines put us up in the airport hotel . . ."

"And . . ."

"We got bored and went swimming . . ."

"Is that what they call it in Denver?" Her mock innocent expression was malicious.

"If you are swimming in a pool full of water . . ."

"I thought you said you were grounded by a blizzard . . ."

"That stayed outside."

"And you were inside . . . swimming. Waste of bloody time, you ask me." She snorted in disgust. "I've given you more credit than you deserve."

224

"At least I wasn't just knitting."

"Should hope to God you weren't. Nothing quicker to put a man off, I'd say, than you quietly knitting. Zzzzhya!" Various parts of her twitched to emphasize her disgust. She'd always vowed she wouldn't knit short of a booby hatch: made her nervous, she said, but she used to watch me for hours in silence if she was troubled. "I see now why it only took you nine days to do this." She patted the Arran and then flipped it into the display basket.

"You don't suppose I knitted my frustrations into it?"

She glanced diffidently at the sweater. "If I get complaints I'll let you know. Who knows? It might guy the wearer up to tremendous performance . . ."

"Better not sell it to the Irish then . . ."

"Oh ho, we are in a state, aren't we? Haven't you heard from him?"

"He doesn't know my address."

"Ssshyoo." She punched the sweater. "Sometimes, Dana, I've no patience with you at all. What was wrong with him? Or was he married?"

So I told her, delighting in the stunned, shocked, surprised and incredulous expressions that floated across her mobile face.

"You don't fool me, Dana Jane, with your self-sacrifice. You're gone on him. You wouldn't have sent him the sweater otherwise. You'll hear from him."

"No."

"You sent him the sweater, didn't you . . ."

"Yes, but . . ."

"Well, he'll write to thank you."

"I didn't put my address on it. I put Tim's."

"Tim's? You clown, you cow, you idiot . . ."

"Look Mairead, the last thing I want is to tie a man up in knots of gratitude . . ."

"That's as good a beginning as many I can think of."

"He's not likely to come here again."

"He's been to Ireland?"

"Something to do with oil."

"Something? Is he an engineer?"

"I think so. I don't know. I don't know that much about him . . ."

"You knew enough to know he didn't murder anybody. Whadd'ya do for three mortal days and nights? Don't answer. I know. But you'd have to talk sometime . . ."

"We did, but not about us."

"Aw, don't get your knickers in a twist . . ." Just then a customer came in the shop which got me off the hook.

Discipline was still the operational word. I disciplined myself to the typewriter by nine-thirty each morning, even if I didn't manage to write much. I caught up on all my correspondence, my filing, my bookkeeping which was a bit of a headache with all the translation of pounds into dollars and back. I could have wished for Tim's calculator or did you call something that sophisticated a pocket computer?

I wandered around the Spring Show, looking dutifully at all the exhibits and seeing most of the pony classes, because of the children. I get some interesting insights at such events, into the kids and the parents. And the ponies are so gorgeous, all dainty stepping and Thelwellian. Of course, DJ was a snow bunny, but I wondered if he'd be pony-crazy if he ever got to Ireland.

Discipline your mind, Dana Jane. DJ!

I caught sight of my face in the mirrors backing one exhibit. Objectively I'm not unpretty. My face bones are good, my complexion has improved with these years in a misty, moisty climate. But, face it, Dana Jane, I told myself cruelly, guys Dan's age would look at gals Mairead's age. Then I envisioned a confrontation between those two and decided they would probably fight like hell. Yet what did I have that would recommend me to someone like Daniel Jerome Lowell?

What was that old New England saying? 'The Cabots speak only to Lowells, and the Lowells speak only to God.' No, I probably had the family names mixed up. But I'd always been amused by the scene evoked: tiered levels with fewer and fewer seats higher up, until the highest two levels where sat the primly clothed Cabots speaking in quiet Back Bay tones to the Lowells above them. And the loftily enthroned Lowells turning with well-bred, but not obsequious,

227

courtesy to the misty-faced figure of the Almighty. Of course, you had no clue as to God's opinion of this chain of command.

My whimsy restored me and I applied conscious discipline to enjoy the rest of my outing that day. There'd been one lad in particular, on a black Welsh pony with bright inquisitive eyes and a curious nose. The lad had had a shock of blond hair and bright inquisitive eyes and the expressions on pony and rider had been so much alike that I marvelled at the match. They'd won a fourth in the working hunter pony and well deserved I felt.

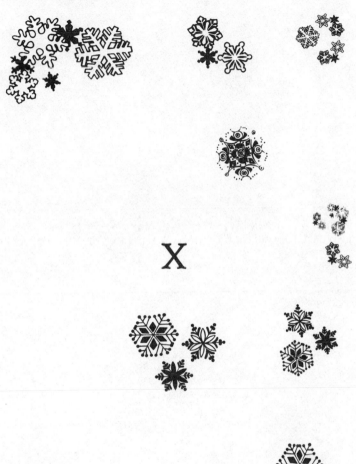

X

TIM GOT HOME! The house was full of noise. Mairead and I met him at Dublin Airport—so did his best friends. I'll never know how the seven of them fit into the Mini. He was tired from the trip for he can never sleep on planes. He was jubilant at his reception. So was I!

He'd lugged home twenty-five of his favorite records as much because he wanted to have his friends hear them as because he didn't want his cousins (he stored his things between terms at my sister's) to scratch his albums. He'd his guitar in the patiently and wildly tape-mended cardboard original case. I ought to buy him a proper one for his birthday this year. He'd only one suitcase and his portable typewriter.

"I was overweight, Mom," he announced joyfully after hugging my ribs in and rubbing my face with whiskery cheeks. "Trish's coming in ten days. Just ten days! Mom, and you know what, I got away with 15 kilos overweight for only $15. And," Tim chortled, "here . . ."

He threw me his ski jacket and I nearly dropped it. It weighed a ton.

"What on earth?"

I felt the lining, crammed with objects that felt like an aerosol can, shoes, a huge wad of something soft that turned out to be a pair of trousers and two pairs of socks, the calculator in one pocket and two packs of playing cards in another . . .

"You must have had twenty pounds in this alone!"

"Right!" and he turned with some urgent questions to Eamonn and Tich. Demanded a kiss from Sheevaun and Mary and Meg and Babs, and socked Pat on the chin. Then he made a big thing of catching Mairead and kissing her.

"One! I told you one was all you'd get from me. You've got other girls here to salute. Bother them!"

"Say, Mom, can I drive home? I got my license."

"Not yet. You're in Ireland, remember?"

"Thank God, thank God!" And he salaamed.

"And . . . you haven't slept all night by the look

of you . . . you drive later . . . when I've had a
chance to change my insurance coverage."

"Now, Mom, I'm . . ."

"I know you're a good careful driver . . . but
later."

We crammed four people in the back of the Peug,
with Mairead beside me, supporting the guitar case.
Tim had managed to get Sheevaun on his lap with
Mary beside him and Eamonn grinning as third. The
trip home was devoted to catching up on all the
gossip, with plans for Trish's entertainment (evidently
Tim had informed all his friends of her imminent
arrival), questions about mutual friends, generally catching up the threads of his life in Ireland.

We dropped the girls off in Blackrock, and then
Eamonn at Shankill. As we reached the Enniskerry
turn-off, Tim sat up, eyes on the road, waiting for the
second turn that would give him a sight of our home.
Our home. We hadn't been in Ireland but four years
and yet this place seemed more homey than any town
in the States: a fact that had impinged on my
consciousness, too. I could experience Tim's feelings
keenly for I'd felt the same way on my return.

I made a decent Irish breakfast for the three of us
and we sat for several hours talking about everything
until I saw Tim struggling to keep his eyes open.

"Look, if your gang is coming back here for tea,
you'd better catch up on your sleep or you'll be no
good to them," I told him and shooed him off to his
room.

233

Anne McCaffrey

He made a token struggle but went off. I followed
in a few moments, to tuck him in, a ritual of his
return even now he was nineteen.

I was planting a kiss on his forehead, when he
caught my hand.

"You left Bethlehem too soon, Mom. You missed
him."

"Missed him?" My innards jolted about. So much
for discipline.

"Yeah, Daniel Jerome."

"What do you mean?"

"He got into Bethlehem Monday evening, Mom.
He was extremely uptight that you'd already left."
Tim's eyes looked deeply into mine. "You know, I'd
thought I'd punch him in the jaw if I ever met him for
getting you in that mess . . ."

"He *wasn't* at fault . . ."

"Ohho!"

"Don't be silly, Tim . . ."

"But, Mom, I couldn't. I liked him. And you
shouldn't have left so fast."

"Oh? I had no reason to hang about. Whatever
possessed him to come to Bethlehem like that?"

Tim gave me one of his shrewd knowing looks.
"Could be he felt he owed you something?"

"For telling the truth?"

Tim arched one eyebrow. "The time, place and
circumstances do make a powerful difference."

"Perhaps. You get some sleep, now, Timothy Raymond Lovell."

234

"I think it was damned nice of him to come in person."

"I agree. I certainly didn't expect it."

"That's obvious." Tim smashed his pillow into submission and flipping on his left side, emphasized his polite wish to follow my original advice and sleep.

I really wanted to find out more details about Dan's visit with Tim. I'd a hundred questions that needed answers, like how had Dan looked? What did he say? Where was he going? How was DJ? Did DJ get the books? (Did he like them?) Had Tim really liked Dan? Yes, Tim had said he did. And he hadn't clobbered him. Not that I would have thought Tim capable of bashing anyone about. So I left Tim to sleep and, as I turned back into the living room, there was Mairead. From the grin on her face, I realized she had overheard the conversation. When she raised one eyebrow, I also realized that my expression gave away my feelings.

"So he came buckety-buckety to see you and you, you bloody ijit, weren't there. Tsck, tsck!"

"Oh, shut up."

"Did Tim mention if he liked the sweater? No, sorry, he wouldn't have got it if you'd only mailed it that day. How far from Bethlehem is Denver?"

"Half a country."

"Wow!"

I was sick with the thought of having missed him and I didn't need Mairead's wise remarks. She caught

235

that, too, and giving my arm a reassuring squeeze, she announced that she had to open the shop, the conquering hero/prodigal's return notwithstanding. She'd be in later. Maybe we'd all go out for a jar.

It was hard not to wake Tim with the assorted questions that sprang to mind to bother me. If Dan had seen Tim, and Tim had liked him, surely Dan could have got my Irish address and written me? More than likely, having made this expensive gesture, and found me departed, he'd salved his own conscience in the matter. I would not dwell on the possible motivation of Daniel Jerome. But it was also curious that Tim had not mentioned Dan's visit in his letters. I'd had three from Tim before he left Lehigh and after Dan's trip. That was odd, indeed. Such reflection robbed me of the passive content I had so narrowly achieved.

I went to the garden and weeded the vegetable rows as penance.

With Tim back, the house began to ring with a loudly-set stereo, the gruff tones of young males raised in friendly fierce debate, the muted tones of Irish girls who surely have the loveliest speaking voices in the world. The blacktopped parking area was crammed with an assortment of motorbikes, respectable cars and chopper pushbikes. Now, however, when I ran out of coffee or milk or bread, there was a cheerful messenger service. And now, also, since most of the young people were employed, I didn't always pay for what was fetched.

Tim had had three very close friends during his years at NewPark Comprehensive: Eamonn and Tich had gone on to University and Pat had entered the family soft goods business. Beyond those three, Tim had a bevy of less intimate acquaintances who apparently were quite willing to make our house their rallying spot. (To give them their due, I'd been approached often during Tim's absence by the boys, asking if they could do any jobs for me.)

If the house was active until wee morning hours, it was also quiet until I had managed to drag Tim from his bed. He has relatively few faults, but rising belatedly out of his downy couch on what he considers his holiday is the prime one. Waking Tim takes roughly three hours, and four cups of coffee, generally consumed cold after much nagging. For particularly urgent matters, a cup of water must be poised in a threatening position above his innocently sleeping face. One douching is all that is needed per week.

I had saved tasks for him, like coping with the weeds at the back of the garden, painting the windowsills, inside and out, where the unkind sun had baked cracks and blisters, recementing certain of the garden steps which frost had loosened, rehanging the garden gate which the winter gales had ripped off its hinges. I used to do such chores myself but with a strapping young man in the house, why should I?

And I wanted them all done before Trish put in her much-discussed appearance or they'd never be accomplished. Tim had marked off the days until her arrival

237

on his calendar, and as the time approached, there was great discussion as to the form her welcome should take. He had borrowed a bike from Eamonn's sister. I had duly finished the tasks he'd given me, but there were other things to be done. Mapping an itinerary, youth hostel cards, awaiting the arrival of the surface-mailed camper foods. He'd had a bit of a job plugging them to his other hiking partners and then began to fret that the packages would not arrive in time. In the face of such anticipation, small wonder that my necessary chores were last on the list of his making.

"June's my holiday, Mom, so please, can't I sleep?"

"This is still May, pet. In June I'll let you sleep."

"I'll be camping in June."

"That's your problem and your holiday. Now it is May."

He got everything done. He always does. And I always have to badger. I also always forget that I have to.

Tim's return had another benefit: I started writing again in earnest. As if the source of my inspiration, the touchstone of the 'Timmy' books, being in residence, sparked my inspiration.

It was very therapeutic to get involved in the intricacies of a book again. It blotted out all other kinds of thinking. I was working at a fair clip, ten to fifteen pages a day, all about a tow-headed boy with a wide blue-eyed face and a black-haired pony with an equally ingenuous face. Then June arrived. And Trish.

Before she moved into the house, I was prepared to resent her for interrupting my concentration with the necessities of hostessing. But Tim knew the way I worked and had evidently explained the process at length to Trish. She fitted into the household routine as if she'd always been there. In the five days Tim allowed her to get synchronized to Irish time before they took off on their bike hike, there was never a dirty cup, plate, spoon or pot in the kitchen. The laundry disappeared the moment it left the body and reappeared neatly ironed and hung, or folded carefully away. She was also not obtrusive in her efforts to help efficiently. I liked her very much, but I worried. She was obviously the sort who made marvellous wives for busy men, but she wanted a career in music. All right, so teaching a school or church group. Tim was just turned 20 and in no position to marry. Maybe they'd be happy to live together for a while? They certainly acted married to my prejudiced eye.

One consolation occurred to me: youth wasn't being wasted by Tim and Trish.

She also got on extremely well with Tim's friends. I presume that Tim had briefed her, or she had extraordinary recall, because she knew exactly who was who, and doing what from the first evening on.

In those five days, my evenings were quiet—all too bloody quiet after three weeks of Tim and his friends. But they had to take Trish to every singing pub in the two counties. And that took some pub crawling.

Trish had not brought her guitar since she allowed

that Tim's was a very good instrument. She had brought, in the lining of her anorak (I wonder who advised her on that?) nine skillion tape blanks. If the typewriter and computer were Tim's favorite appendages, the tape recorder and mike were hers. I wondered if she slept with them. No, cancel that, Dana.

The day before their scheduled departure was madsville: tents, the campers' dehydrated and flash frozen, vacuum-packed food arrived and were admired, haversacks, bike packs, boots, pans, all the paraphernalia occupied my living room. Everything was weighed so that no one carried more than was bearable. There was a huge argument between Trish and Tim because she wanted to carry as much weight as he: she was just as fit, wasn't she, and not a scrawny wight. He was being a male chauvinist pig, that's what, and she wouldn't permit it. I think Sheevaun and Mary wished she'd be quiet about equality: they were quite willing for Eamonn and Pat to take the heavier loads.

Tim solved the problem by saying Trish could carry their tent one day, and he the next.

We had a huge feast and booze-up the night before, though it ended, on Tim's orders, at midnight, to allow for a good sleep and an early start. They'd have to take it easy the first day, possibly the second, but an early start would mean they could have more rests the first day, to limber muscles unused during the winter. (After those hills in Lehigh, I wouldn't have thought he needed any limbering so I think he meant Eamonn and the girls. I knew that Pat had biked to Belfield from Shankill every day.)

Mairead and her new man came, on Tim's invitation. Nick had done a good deal of cycling so he fit into the evening far better than Mairead, to judge by her bemused expression, had anticipated. Nick Hewlett was a sort of nondescript-looking person until he smiled or until you had talked him up a bit. He tended to hold his own counsel, which must certainly recommend him to Mairead who resented gratuitous advice, but he knew a great many things about travelling in Ireland. Not surprising when I finally asked him what was his business and found he'd been chauffeuring for one of the big hire-car firms. He often took on assignments with film companies and he had a store of amusing tales to tell about driving this or that big name film star. He'd been assigned to the *Rafferty's Daughter* crew so he had a good deal of pertinent information to give Trish, with names of people to look up·for more than the average courtesies.

"Where'd you find him?" I asked Mairead on the side.

"Let's just say, we found each other."

"Did you know all that?"

"No, but then," and she shot it back at me, "we didn't talk about us."

That set both of us off laughing and neither of us could explain to the others.

The evening was great fun and I tried not to think of tomorrow. As I'd dreaded, the house was all the

Anne McCaffrey

more empty for their leaving. Tim's a good orga-
nizer and despite my attempts to stuff everyone with
pancakes enough to last the week, much less the first
morning, they mounted their bikes, festooned with
oddments of equipment at exactly seven o'clock. They
looked mighty ungainly, bending over the handlebars,
their backpacks bulging, as they pumped down the
road, two by two, and out of my sight.

Tim had promised to give me a shout now and
then, so I'd know they hadn't come to any grief. I'd
that much to look forward to.

I occupied that day with housecleaning: I couldn't
leave all the bits and pieces out or Mrs. Munday
would hide them on Tuesday when she came and
we'd never find anything. I also restocked the freezer
which had been severely depleted.

Mairead phoned me as I was sitting down to a
lonely dinner of chicken wings, and she and Nick
took me out for a few jars. Nick had enough stories to
fill a book of 'Timmy's' if such stories had been fit
for young eyes. I'd never realized that film stars
could be so . . . so . . . human?

I crawled into bed that night, too well oiled to care
about anything except closing my watering eyes. They
could have a smokeless room in some of the bigger
pubs, couldn't they, for the people like me? They
have smokeless sections of airplanes, don't they?

The next morning was worse. I marched myself
back upstairs at nine-thirty and sat dutifully at the
typewriter. The story absented itself as if Tim's pres-

242

ence had been responsible for its progress and it was suspended until he returned in three weeks.

Three weeks in a doubly empty house? And Mairead far too involved with Nick to want to share his company? I would go absolutely stark raving bonkers.

I noticed glumly that the calendar said it was D-Day. Deserted Day, I grembled to myself. I was on my fourth cup of coffee. Mr. Murphy had brought only circular mail, sent surface from the States. It was fund-raising time for colleges so I didn't even have anything palatable to browse through with my coffee. Or answer later, thus disposing of more heavy time. Injury upon insult!

The doorbell purred and then someone applied the knocker vigorously to the door as if they didn't trust mechanical devices.

"I'm coming! I'm coming!"

I wondered who the hell would be so insistent. And then ran, because, maybe something had happened to Tim and Trish, and it was the Gardai . . .

I hauled open the door and stared.

Leaning indolently against the doorjamb was Daniel Jerome Lowell, his mouth twitching in echo of the pure devilment in his serge-blue eyes.

"What are *you* doing here?"

I clung to the door handle so as not to throw my arms about his neck, sternly telling myself that I'd've been glad to see anyone who wasn't the bearer of bad tidings.

The light went out of his eyes. I know I had

sounded shrewish with relief, but I was trying not to sound overjoyed, too. Nothing more certain to put a man off . . .

I grabbed his hand and pulled him over the threshold.

"Tim and Trish left yesterday on their bikes . . ." I said in a rush of explanation. "And the way you . . . summoned me . . . I was scared stiff it was the Gardai reporting an accident. Don't stand there! Come in. When did you get here? Oh, you've a car. Why didn't you phone? I'd've picked you up at the airport. Are you staying long? I didn't mean to sound inhospitable or . . ."

Baggins came charging out of the bushes to inspect the newcomer and the awkwardness of my greeting was covered by necessary introductions. I wasn't surprised that Baggins liked Dan and lick-kissed him. I'd've been more surprised if Baggins had been aggressive.

"I got in this morning," Dan said, still ruffling Baggins' neck fur, "I don't know how long I'm staying and I didn't mean to alarm you. I need a car for transport so I didn't phone you and you're a marvellous dog, aren't you, Baggins?"

Baggins promptly produced more ecstasies of welcome, wriggling between Dan's legs so that he almost tripped Dan up.

"Would you like some coffee, Dan?"

"I'd love some . . ."

". . . Or breakfast?"

"I'd in mind to invite you out to lunch . . ."

"Good heavens, what time is it?"

"Nearly twelve . . ."

"But you must be exhausted if you came in on that morning flight."

"I'm used to flying."

"I'll fix the coffee. I won't be a minute . . ." I got out of the room, so flustered that I dropped the kettle into the sink as I tried to fill it. The fluster that descended to my innards and my hands shook so that I spilled coffee as I filled the filter top, dropped a coffee mug, fortunately only into the plastic dish drainer so it was unscathed.

"This place is just right for you, Jenny," he said, appearing in the archway from the dining room. "Had it long?"

"Three years now." Yes, yes, talk inanities until you can get your breath back. "You're sure you don't want an egg and some good Irish bacon?"

"I said I wanted to take you out to lunch . . ."

He really was in my kitchen, the warm orange of the walls making his tanned face darker. He looked much less haggard than he had the last time I'd seen him. In Denver, in Peter's living room. His hair was shorter, though, and he'd trimmed the moustache recently. The casual shirt, open at his throat, the dark blue blazer made his presence all the more overpowering for me.

"Unless you've something else planned . . ."

"No, Tim and Trish left yesterday on their trip . . ."

"I know . . ."

"How do you know?"

"You just told me," and he jerked his hand backwards toward the front of the house and then he grinned, coming towards me. "Besides, Tim told me he and Trish would be gone by the sixth . . ." Dan moved across the small room, towards me.

"Tim told you?"

"Yes, when I came to Bethlehem. Only you'd already hightailed it out of the States . . ."

I swallowed. To think I had missed him by such a small margin. "I had no reason to remain. My tour was over. Tim and I had had our visit. I was anxious to get home . . ."

If he didn't move away from me, six weeks of careful discipline, or stern exorcism . . .

He did move, but not away. Closer. He leaned against the counter, facing me, and before I could turn away from his gaze, he had caught my chin and tipped my face up.

"Jenny," he said and folded me into his arms because he'd seen the ridiculous watering of my eyes. "Jenny, Jenny!" And he kissed my cheek and stroked my hair, not at all the way Tim does, and loved me with his hands and the length of his body while I stupidly bawled away the longing and frustration of the last six weeks.

"Jenny! Jenny?" He framed my face with both hands and kissed me slowly, ever so slowly, leisurely as if he had all the time in the world.

Except I'd put the kettle on and it's the whistling kind.

He didn't interrupt the kiss but with one hand, he let go of me and tried to find the kettle. He burned his hand and that broke the kiss.

I was all contrition but my weeps had turned to laughter as I held his burned fingers under the cold water. I got command of myself.

"You'll freeze my fingers off," he complained, pulling his hand out of mine and examining the red marks critically.

"He who pulls kettle from fire without watchful eye gets fingers burned! I've something to take the sting out . . ."

He snatched me back to his side. "Jenny, *are* you glad to see me?"

Our eyes met and he slowly dropped his hand, his expression puzzled and expectant. Or hopeful? My behavior had blighted him. He must have come straight from the airport to my house. Tim had obviously given him precise directions for how else could he have found the house? His eyes were weary, too, from travel fatigue and the time change, and anxious.

Slowly I became aware that his anxiety was real: he was very unsure of his welcome. I had attributed to him more self-confidence and assurance than I now realized he possessed. The murder charge had been a terrible, terrible strain and he had not recovered from that either.

"Did you know that it's D-Day?" I asked with the first steadying thought that had come to my mind.

He blinked in an effort to follow my line of thought.

"I was grembling about the house, full of self-pity when you knocked, banged and clattered at my door like the knell of doom. I'd decided that 'D' is for Deserted. Now I guess it's really 'D' for Dan Day."

I'd said the right thing. The anxiety cleared out of his face and his eyes began to sparkle as I remembered they could from Denver. Lightly he put his arms around my waist, wincing a bit as he inadvertently clasped the burned fingers.

"Tim told me that I should come the day after he and Trish left because you'd be feeling deserted and I could . . ." He broke off with a laugh.

"Catch me with my defenses down?"

"That's right." He nodded vigorously, his face smiling. "I thought he was wrong at first until . . ." He hugged me to him, swaying both of us back and forth. "Oh, Jenny!" And he buried his face in my hair, nibbling at my neck.

Resolutely I pushed him from me, and miraculously he let me.

"Yes, Jenny, we need to talk. Seriously. So make me that coffee which has scarred me for life."

Dan perched on one of the breakfast stools as I poured water into the filter top, got out the sugar and milk, added another cup to the one I had nearly broken.

"So, why besides making it a 'D' for Dan Day, are you in Dublin?"

"I'm here to see you, Jenny."

"I thought you were doing something about off-shore oil."

"I'm here to see you, first and foremost, Jenny."

"Where's DJ?" I was scared of why he wanted to see me, first and foremost.

"In Denver with the Taggerts. I wanted him to finish school before . . . Before I made other plans for him."

He took the cup I offered, lifting it in a salute.

"He's had a very rough two years, Jenny . . . If I'd had any idea that he was being so abused . . ."

"Abused?" I got absolutely rigid with hatred of a woman who'd abuse a nice youngster like DJ. I thought of his sensitive face, the haunted eyes, the intensity of his stare when he measured me up as the person who could absolve his father.

"Not physically," Dan hastily reassured me, "but I've a lot to make up to him. By the way, Tim's a credit to you. I'd've known him anywhere from those books."

"You haven't ever read them?"

"DJ insisted," and Dan smiled again, this time pure mischief at my shock. "And I'll admit that I thoroughly enjoyed them. Them and a second childhood. Tim and DJ got on very well, by the way . . ."

"Tim and DJ?" I sank, strengthless, onto the other stool.

"Yes, when DJ found I was going to Bethlehem, he insisted on coming with me. He wanted to thank you, too . . ."

"Oh, Dan, if I'd only known. He must have been so disappointed."

"Not half as much as I was but then, he met Tim," Dan went on blandly. "DJ said for me to tell you he'd've known Tim anywhere, too. And I was to say that Tim in person is even nicer than Tim in the books."

"Except when you want to get him up in the morning to do chores."

Dan laughed. "And thanks for that sweater, Jenny."

"You did get it? Did it fit?"

"I have it with me. That's why I came."

"Why you came? But you said it fit?"

"So it does. But I had to come, you see, because you'd sent me the sweater."

I was confused.

"Why would that make you come? I mean, I did hope to get a note from you saying that it had come . . ."

"I wanted to write, but after I'd talked to Tim . . ."

"But you couldn't have got the sweater that fast . . ."

"I've had quite a few conversations with Tim, Jenny," he said gently, "because I wasn't going to appear where I wasn't wanted."

"Wasn't wanted?"

He put down his coffee mug and I could see that his expression was wary.

"Look, Jenny, I'd had to involve you in a very messy business. I wasn't at all sure if you ever wanted to see or hear from me again. I sure as hell couldn't have blamed you. And that night at Pete's . . . it seemed to me that you couldn't wait to get out of the house when you discovered I was there."

"I only left because I didn't want to give the D.A. . . ."

"I know that now, Jenny, but that evening . . . I'd been through such hell . . ."

"Oh, Dan . . ." I took his hands in mine.

"And to see you, so tired . . . so . . . And thinking about DJ and Pete's two girls . . ." He rubbed at his hair, grimacing against the memory of that desperate time. "Then you up and leave the States, goddamn near as soon as you'd got the all-clear from Pete. I was sure you'd never want to set eyes on me again. And Tim didn't give me a very warm welcome, either. Until he saw DJ . . ." Dan managed a little grin.

I was appalled by Tim's duplicity. "Why, the brat. He didn't mention a thing. If I'd known you'd come . . ."

"I asked Tim not to tell you. DJ and I went back to Denver. Tim did say that he didn't think you held any bad feelings for me . . ."

"I didn't. I didn't. . . ." His turn to hold hands for reassurance.

"And then the sweater came. Jenny, I've thought and thought. I've tried to convince myself that it's

251

only gratitude, that it's because you are the antithesis of Noreen Sue and this is reboundsville. But Jenny, I can't get you out of my mind. What in hell should we do about it?''

He was appealing to me, his eyes, his warm hands, his whole body leaning towards me across the counter. And why in hell did it have to be in the way? For a long moment, I couldn't answer, couldn't do anything because of the upsurge of emotion, all joyful and mixed with the primitive response of his presence.

''I think we should talk about it . . .''

''Then you don't dislike me . . .''

''Whatever gave you any notion that I did?''

''That's my Jenny!''

''No, don't get any nearer. We have to be rational, sensible . . .''

''Why?'' and he was nibbling sexily at my left palm and wrist. ''I didn't fly three thousand miles to be sensible. I came because I wanted you, I wanted to see you and talk with you and be with you. And I'm selfish, I want DJ to have you, too. And DJ to have someone like Tim in the background, to help erase the darkness of these last two years.'' He was pressing my fingers into his palm, one at a time, enumerating the various points. ''You've a profession, so have I. The two professions are not mutually exclusive. I've the house in Denver, you've one here. We could even manage to spend a half year in each country. And Tim says he'd love to learn to ski . . .''

I thought of the blond boy on the black pony and how I'd wondered if DJ would like one.

"I want you, Jenny, for myself and for DJ. You have what we both happen to stand in grave need of: integrity, understanding and compassion. Those qualities come over in your books, you know. And I can trust you. I think that's the prime consideration. I know I can trust you. You knew what even my best friends, Pete included, did not know: that I couldn't, wouldn't, and didn't take a life."

"But I *knew* that. I was there!"

His grip tightened almost painfully. "Jenny, even before Pete told you when the murder was supposed to have happened, you told him I hadn't done it."

"Didn't Pete believe you?" I was incredulous and yet . . .

Dan shook his head, smiling sadly. "Pete's been in the business too long to trust anybody, anymore. Only you and DJ believed in me. I need you, Jenny, because I can trust you, because I want DJ to realize that he can trust someone again. And if you think that trust, need, respect and . . ." here that impossible quirk of devilment gleamed in his eyes again, "the most agreeable rapport in bed . . . aren't the basis for a lasting relationship . . . Jenny, couldn't we just try it on for size this summer? Tim was blunt that I should ask you . . . Couldn't we see if it wouldn't work on a more permanent basis. . . ."

There was that in his attitude that told me he was ready right then to marry me. He rose, still holding my hands as he came round the corner. All discipline deserted me. I had only a few seconds more of rational thought because the moment he started to kiss me . . .

"Couldn't we, please, Jenny?"

"I rather think we'd better . . ."

I could tell myself later that it was the challenge of erasing the haunted look in DJ's eyes but, when Dan's lips covered mine, I knew that it was to remove, forever, the anxiety in Dan's.